D

Dr Lydia Richmond and her ex-husband Lance were still on friendly terms after their divorce, even to the extent of working together in the same general practice. In fact, they were better friends now than they had been while still married. Then, to Lydia's dismay, Lance announced that he was getting married again. . .

Sonia Deane is a widow with one son, lives in the Cotswolds, and has written over 120 books. The Doctor Nurse stories were fortuitous. She chose a doctor hero and from then her readers wanted a medical background. Having personal friends who are doctors enables Sonia Deane's research to be verified. She has also been out with an ambulance team and donned a white coat in hospital. Her previous novels include *Doctor's Romance, Doctor's Forbidden Love* and *Doctor Deceived*.

DOCTOR'S LOVE AFFAIR

BY
SONIA DEANE

MILLS & BOON LIMITED
15-16 BROOK'S MEWS
LONDON W1A 1DR

*First published in Great Britain 1987
by Mills & Boon Limited*

© Sonia Deane 1987

*Australian copyright 1987
Philippine copyright 1987
This edition 1987*

ISBN 0 263 75721 8

*Set in Monotype Times 10.7 on 11.3 pt.
03-0487-49055*

*Typeset in Great Britain by
Associated Publishing Services
Printed and bound in Great Britain by
Collins, Glasgow*

CHAPTER ONE

SURGERY was nearly over, and the drowsiness of the early June day in London's Connaught Square made Lydia relax and look at her employer, Dr Lance Richmond, as she said, 'I've been your locum for six months.' Her voice held an element of surprise. She found the fact intriguing.

'And we've been divorced for nearly a year,' he added reflectively. 'To be honest, we've never been such good friends, not even when we first married.'

There was a pause before she hastened, aware of the incongruity of the situation, 'That was three years ago—this month, to be exact.' A somewhat provocative smile touched her lips. 'I shall never know why I left hospital and became your locum to tide you over after Keith (Lance's partner) died so suddenly.'

'A willingness to help lame dogs!'

'You don't fit the description.'

They were an attractive couple—she twenty-six, a light brunette, with a glamour inherited from a romantic maternal grandmother, plus an artistic flair handed down by her delightful, impecunious artist father who died at fifty, penniless, though successful and happy. Her mother had survived him for just three years. Lydia's eyes could flash, beguile and challenge.

Lance, at thirty-three, was tall, strong and powerful. He had a charm that was natural and a personality that dwarfed lesser men. Women were immediately attracted to him, and he stimulated that attraction by his deceptive indifference.

'You know, Lydia,' he went on smoothly, 'it's amazing how clearly one can see a picture when standing back from it. If we're frank, we were never really sexually compatible.'

Lydia bristled, without betraying the fact. The summing up seemed an affront.

'A mutual disadvantage,' she suggested, a faint edge to her voice.

'Oh, true,' he agreed with infuriating reasonableness.

The mood changed as she said with acerbity, 'None of that matters now; all we need to do is to work harmoniously, although I'm sure you realize I shall be moving on before very long. You've dithered over getting another partner, and you certainly cannot run this practice on your own.'

Lance studied her disarmingly, realising that he had settled into the habit of her being there, so much so that the possibility of her going came as a shock. She was right, of course, he argued to himself, and mumbled about having someone in mind, asking abruptly, 'Will you move out of London?'

At the time of the divorce Lydia had remained in their joint mews flat near Porchester Place, while Lance had taken a furnished one actually in Connaught Square, so that they were both on the spot so far as the practice was concerned. The practice itself was run from Carisbrooke House, a large Georgian building overlooking the Square gardens, and tenanted by other doctors; with a central reception area, switchboard and small staff to direct patients to their particular practitioner. Had the money been available they could have made it into a thriving centre, housing all modern equipment, thus sparing patients the long treks and waiting at the various hospitals. As it was they were able, to a degree, to take advantage of the diverse skills of their on-the-spot colleagues. Lance's rooms housed himself, Lydia, the practice nurse, Ruby Webster, Mrs Trent, his secretary—a plump jolly sixty-year-old who had been with him for five years ever since he started at Carisbrooke—and Julie Marsden, recently appointed as receptionist and eminently satisfactory, with her somewhat challenging sexuality and sympathetic, faintly humorous manner. They were on the ground floor, so that she was spared many journeys in the lift, dealing with nervous patients, or the infirm, incapable of managing alone.

'Yes.' Lance's words, 'sexually incompatible', echoed, making Lydia feel inadequate. She had not given consideration to that aspect of their relationship, which had appeared to be normal. Their failure generally, she had argued, lay in their clashing opinions and diverse emotional reactions. Lance seemed to live in a private world, to which he never gave her the key, and she hated the isolation. They were too modern to suffer in silence, or wish to plough through years of unhappiness to make a marriage work; a marriage they had finally agreed had been a mistake in the first place. But out of all the upheaval and general chaos, friendship remained. Perhaps, the thought struck her, Lance's assessment was correct after all: had they *been* sexually compatible, they would hardly have adjusted to this present pedestrian relationship, which they enjoyed on a platonic working basis.

They studied each other speculatively.

'You don't look twenty-six,' he said suddenly and abruptly. 'Nothing like it, although one obviously knows you must be a certain age to have qualified and be practising.'

'And you don't look thirty-three,' she countered, 'although you have an air of experience.'

He laughed. 'Just as well in my job. . . you're very attractive, Lydia. More so, now, than ever. Perhaps you, too, have benefited from experience.'

It struck her that Lance would never have made such a remark during their marriage, his attitude being, 'You *know* I think you're attractive, or I shouldn't have married you'.

'One can benefit from experience, but whether I've *learned* from it,' she countered with a smile, 'is another matter.'

'I should say that the two of necessity go hand in hand. . . hell, we're getting serious!'

His deep attractive voice broke on a chuckle and she became suddenly aware of him. The bright summer light focused his deep cream linen jacket, revealing a blue shirt and discreet tie. His tall slim body was athletic without any muscular disadvantages to coarsen the overall effect. Memories crowded back. It was impossible to believe that once she had been his wife. Nostalgia made her suddenly selfconscious.

The intercom went and Mrs Trent's voice was urgent, 'Oh, Doctor, it's Mrs Hall! She hasn't an appointment, but she's in a dreadful state.'

Lance, startled, said immediately, 'Send her in.'

Trudy Hall, whom they knew as a friendly acquaintance, came in head down, almost cowering, and murmuring, 'I'm so sorry. . . but I was afraid— really afraid.'

She was a pretty dark-haired woman of thirty-five. Now, one eye was blackened, her upper lip swollen, while an angry scarlet weal disfigured her cheek.

'Good God!' Lance and Lydia looked horrified. He asked urgently, 'What's happened?'

She seemed to crumple up in the patients' chair, her sudden calm alarming, her voice broken and hopeless.

'It was Neville—he—'

'Your *husband*—' gasped Lance, immediately proceeding to examine her to make sure that there was no eye injury, or damage to the head. Lydia prepared a cold compress.

Trudy gave a heartrending little cry.

'I couldn't keep it to myself any longer,' she said desperately. 'But his temper was so frightening.'

Lance and Lydia exchanged glances, both stunned.

Lance echoed, 'Temper? He's the last man—' He stopped at what he knew to be empty words, because every drama happened to that 'last' man, or woman.

'That's what everyone thinks, and why I've been able to deceive people for the twelve years we've been married.'

'But why didn't you come to me before? Go to the police?' Lance was almost belligerent because he could hardly control his anger, knowing that Trudy Hall was a reliable, truthful woman whose word could be relied upon.

Trudy caught her breath. 'I could never go to the police,' she said almost apologetically. 'You see, the trouble is that I love him, and so many of the twelve years we've been married have been good years.' She spoke with a deep earnestness. 'And you've never suspected that he had a—a temper, or that he could be violent?'

Lance was appalled. He had regarded Neville Hall as an astute, successful—which he was—chartered surveyor, whose manner was indicative of normality and kindliness—the cliché, 'He wouldn't hurt a fly', being the biggest misconception of all.

'Never,' he admitted, feeling almost guilty. 'He was so concerned when you had your appendix out, and always so considerate—'

'And he *is*. That's what makes it such hell,' Trudy explained.

'I'd like him to have a brain scan,' Lance said forcefully, while realising that the pattern over twelve years was unlikely to betray a brain tumour.

'He would *never* have treatment of any kind, because he would never admit that he needed it. Apart from you, he hates doctors and is very anti-medicine.' She was growing calmer as she spoke; trembling less, courage returning.

'Is there anything that triggers off these attacks?'

'Anything that thwarts him. This time it was a question of whether we went to the cinema, or stayed at home to watch a wild life programme which I enjoy. It's almost as though I ought not to *want* to do anything that doesn't conform to his wishes. I'd only been married a few months when he slapped my face. Afterwards he had an aggrieved air, self-pitying; and in the end it was I who felt in the wrong. I— I have to pander to him. It's the only way. Sometimes he just raves. . . he doesn't often do—do *this*, but when he does I feel sick and degraded—mostly with myself for not having the courage to leave him. His behaviour is the dark secret that haunts my life. I can't *tell* anyone. . . but this time something seemed to snap and here I am. . . but I'm better now,' Trudy insisted.

'If I could have a talk with him,' suggested Lance. 'Psychiatric treatment—'

'The very word would be an affront, and he'd *never* talk. It may be months before he—he does this again,' she said, plunging into the inevitable defence. 'I'm sure he's sorry afterwards.' It was a pathetic apology.

'Does he say so?'

'Not in so many words,' she said loyally, 'but I know he is.'

'But he's not ill; hasn't any physical symptoms? Doesn't complain of headaches, or—'

'Nothing like that, except that he—he sometimes goes to bed for no reason.'

'Playing on your sympathy,' Lance said gravely. 'Listen, Trudy; you can't live the rest of your life pandering to a man you're afraid of. *Something* must be done.'

She answered in a whisper, 'And I can't live the rest of my life without him. I'm sorry. . . I must seem to be wasting your time, coming here, weak, panicking and then refusing your help. But I know him, you see, and no one else does. . . he's faithful, generous and good to me in so many ways.' She covered her face with her hands, ignoring the compress, as though ashamed of her own emotional weakness, adding pathetically, 'And he loves me. . . he *does*—in his way.'

Lance knew there was no hope of his using his professional skill when it was not desired, any more than the police could act without the consent of the wife in such cases. It was a familiar, tragic pattern, but human nature did not change, and the loyalty of woman was beyond comprehension.

'One thing I *can* do,' he said forcefully, 'is to call in from time to time on a friendly basis. I've done so before on rare occasions, and we sometimes meet socially. From now on we must strengthen that bond, so I can keep an eye on you.'

Trudy said, immediately apprehensive, 'But don't call too soon after—after this, or   might suspect.' She could not bring herself to add that when Neville was in one of his tempers he would not be ashamed if the Queen witnessed his degradation, neither would he apologise.

It struck Lydia that it was like trying to treat an unacknowledged alcoholic without hospitalisation, or the drying-out process.

Lance told her gravely, 'You must be absolutely honest with me, Trudy: have these attacks ever come within the scope of brutal assault, as distinct from superficial cuts and bruises, as now, and for which there's very little that can be done?'

She didn't hesitate. 'Never; or I should have had to come to you sooner, shouldn't I?'

He was convinced.

'But how do you explain these cuts and bruises to your friends?'

'Almost as a joke. Neville stresses the fact that I'm accident-prone and we laugh about it. I can always make up a story, and we haven't so many friends that I can't put off seeing the few we have. I even stock up with food—I've a deep-freeze—so I never need to go *out* shopping, and in any case, Neville is very good at it.'

Lance felt utterly hopeless and dismayed. Lydia, watching him, sensed his anxiety and frustration.

'And,' Trudy hastened to add, 'it isn't as if this was a regular occurrence. The fear of it happening is worse than the reality. But I sometimes reach a pitch. . . well, I'm always watching him, apprehensive—'

'Like a mother with a difficult child?'

She dropped her gaze in abject agreement. 'I suppose I shouldn't know how to live a—a normal life. . . yet if I wanted anything, he'd go to any lengths to get it for me.' She sighed deeply. 'You think I should leave him, don't you?'

Lance knew her desperation. And Lydia knew that she didn't want an impossibility confirmed.

'It's your life, your marriage. I just hate not being able to help,' Lance replied.

'You have, by listening. Now I have someone who understands and with whom I've been honest. Keeping a situation to oneself can be so nerve-racking.' Trudy added quietly, 'He'd go to pieces without me—' She made a little apologetic gesture.

Lance knew she was already feeling guilty and embarrassed for having come to see him and betrayed a secret she had kept for twelve years. The Nevilles of this world had the power to engender that quality. Confirming this belief, as she got to her feet she sighed, 'I—I feel ashamed for having. . . worried you. I don't know why I was so frightened this time, but the strain. . . I daren't give way.' She added, sensing their anxiety, 'But I shall be all right. . . he'll have a hard-done-by attitude and won't ask me where I've been. I always get in the car and drive around. It's a kind of sanctuary—like it is here.' She gazed at the high-ceilinged room, the large windows overlooking the Square. Sunlight streamed in through the net curtains, falling on Lance's mahogany desk, instrument cabinet, and the comfortable high-backed leather chairs, upholstered in dark red. Then she looked from face to face, knowing their own story, wondering why two such charming, normal people couldn't have made their marriage work. The juxtaposition with her own seemed ironic.

'Thank you for seeing me,' she said simply. 'I know you have an appointment system and Nurse Webster was very understanding in getting Mrs Trent to speak to you. It's past six now, and surgery's over. I didn't overlook the fact that it began at four-thirty.'

Lance and Lydia knew that she was talking merely to boost her courage to face up to what lay ahead.

Lydia saw her to her car. Passers-by looked and then turned away, fearful of causing embarrassment as they saw the bruising on Trudy's face. The hot summer sunshine, the bright green of the trees in the Square and the deep blue of the cloudless sky seemed to mock the misery that hung like a ghost about that pitiful slim figure.

'Don't forget,' Lydia insisted, 'that we're only a matter of minutes in the car from your flat and you've only to ring—any time.'

Trudy put out a hand and touched Lydia's. 'Thank you,' she whispered, tears gushing to her eyes, making the discoloured one seem even more pathetic. 'Talking to you. . . it will make it less lonely. . . A burden becomes so heavy when you carry it alone, and you have to do so *much* that no one understands.'

'You can always talk to us,' Lydia promised, the plural coming naturally because, she told herself, of the professional association.

The car drove away and Lydia went back into the house. Nurse Webster said, as Lydia entered the front door, 'I knew you and Dr Richmond would want to see Mrs Hall.' It was an explanation, because the case would normally have been left to her to deal with.

Ruby Webster's face was gentle and beautiful. In her uniform she looked the epitome of youth—happy youth. She was engaged to a doctor, had a stable home background, and was to be married in the spring, continuing with her job. Lydia felt a sudden and unexpected envy. Her own mood, despite Trudy Hall, was that of inexplicable restlessness as she returned to Lance's consulting room.

'We ought never to be surprised by anything,' she said flatly, 'but I'm staggered. . . Would psychiatry help?'

'Nothing can help a patient who won't acknowledge that he needs help, and I can do nothing without his wife's sanction. There's an inadequacy somewhere; an inherent weakness. . . Amazing that she can still love him and want to preserve their marriage.'

There was a moment of silence during which Lance looked at Lydia with an intimacy greater than they had known for a very long while.

She introduced a personal note unwittingly, as she said swiftly, 'We couldn't even adjust to temperamental differences.'

Tension, new and a little unnerving, surged between them. The muted roar of London's traffic seemed to add to the silence, rather like a challenge.

'No,' he said, 'we couldn't settle for second best, and I can't see much virtue in a situation like the Halls', even though I admire her.' His voice deepened in faint challenge. 'If that's an example of marriage, I don't want any part of it.'

She burst out involuntarily, 'Or *any* part of marriage. We were agreed on that!'

His gaze was disarming. 'True. . . freedom is a magic word.' He stood there, his masculinity a temptation. *Sexually incompatible*. The words returned mockingly and she wondered if he had found that compatibility with any other woman since their divorce. They never discussed their personal affairs, and while she realised that women, generally, sought him out, she had no means of knowing if there was any special attraction in his life.

'I must get back to my room,' she said somewhat abruptly, just as Una Mercer, the health visitor attached to the practice, came in, after Mrs Trent's assurance that the coast was clear. She was a former hospital Sister and had a brisk efficiency tempered with sympathy and understanding, escaping any domineering air. She was thirty, unmarried from choice, with deep brown eyes, both gentle and flashing. She came straight to the point.

'Old Mrs Cranford,' she said. 'As you know, she hasn't any relatives, braves it out alone, and never grumbles.'

Lance exclaimed swiftly, 'I've great respect for Mrs Cranford.'

'She needs a visit. Bad cold; and her small room in her tiny flat is, or seems to be, about ninety. No air. If we could get her into hospital. . .' She paused eloquently, her gaze meeting Lance's in mute appeal.

'I think,' he said firmly, 'this is where something can be done. Mrs Cranford has been my patient ever since I came here.'

Una's expression of relief was obvious. 'Could we meet there in half an hour? I must look in on your young Mrs Gorton, just out of hospital with her first baby. But she's only in Upton Street—'

'Half an hour,' he agreed.

She nodded and hurried away.

Lydia returned to her room, which was small, but had a welcoming air rather than an austere one. The house was taking to itself the peace of evening, when doctors and staff hurried out of the building to their respective cars, the few remaining with late appointments, lost in the labyrinth of empty corridors and lifts when they finally departed. Lydia cleared her desk, said goodbye to Mrs Trent, Nurse Webster and Julie, and waited for Lance to return from Mrs Cranford, anxious to know the result of the visit.

He came in, solemn but relieved.

'We got her admitted to St Joseph's Nursing Home,' he told her. 'I was lucky, Dickie Jameson was on emergencies and did a bit of manoeuvring.'

'How is she?'

'She'll die in comfort and dignity,' he said quietly, 'and that's the least we can do for her at eighty-four.' He hurried on, 'All packed up?'

'Yes. I stayed to finish off some personal letters. I knew you had a late appointment and would be back.' Lydia smiled and changed the mood. '*You're* on call tonight.'

'Gadding about?' It was a question, stimulated by the implication of her remark.

'If you put having dinner with Steven in that category—yes.'

'Steven!' There was a note of indifference in the utterance.

Steven Telford was a solicitor and had been a friendly acquaintance during their marriage. He had not disappeared into the shadows after the divorce, as people were apt to do.

'You were never very keen on Steven,' Lydia said conversationally.

'We hadn't a great deal in common. I'm not particularly interested in the law, and he's not interested in medicine.'

'But his family and yours have been friends—'

'Oh, yes,' Lance cut in. . . 'solicitors and physicians! But my father still deals with Steven's father, as you know. Henry Telford ought to have gone to the Bar.'

'And your father should have become a consultant,' Lydia reflected.

'He's happier being a G.P. in Hampstead, with his partner. . . will you be coming over on Sunday, by the way?'

Lance's parents, Edward and Marion Richmond, kept open house on Sunday mornings, and Lydia had remained part of the family despite the divorce. Marion and she were fast friends, and Marion had been desperately sorry when the marriage broke up, but had been wise enough not to interfere; she and Edward maintaining that friendship was the cement that would perpetuate harmony and give support in any emergency. Marion was a plump, motherly woman, well-dressed rather than smart, with a clear skin and bright welcoming eyes, who loved cooking and everything to do with homemaking. She had happily devoted her married life to her husband, Lance and his brother Philip, who was at the moment in Australia on an engineering project. They lived in a rambling old house overlooking the Heath; a house which had been in the family for three generations, but was of no particular architectural importance.

'Yes,' Lydia said brightly. 'I love Sundays at Heath Edge.' She looked at Lance, her eyes smiling. 'Thank heaven we've proved that divorced people can remain good friends.'

'*Just* good friends,' he chuckled.

The front door bell sounded like an alarm through the now deserted house.

'That will be my patient, Mr Kempton.'

'I'll see him in,' Lydia said instantly. 'What's a locum for?' She reached the door. 'I've got letters to finish, so I'll probably see you before you leave. I'm not meeting Steven until eight-thirty.'

'Lydia?' Lance's voice was urgent.

'Yes?'

'Don't get too fond of him; he's no more right for you than I was!'

She flashed, 'I must be a very fastidious lady!'

'You are—that's the trouble.'

She hurried through the main hall, past the now unmanned switchboard and reception desk; Lance went to his consulting room.

Was she fastidious? she asked herself, as she opened the door to a rather nervous, breathless little man of fifty, who had domestic problems and a mistress who found his bank balance the attraction, but had no desire to change the status quo, while he was, ironically, prepared to wreck his life in order to get a divorce and marry her.

'Good evening, Doctor,' he said a trifle nervously. 'I—'

'Dr Richmond will see you at once,' Lydia said reassuringly, knowing that he had not expected to be greeted by her. 'The staff have all gone,' she explained.

'Yes; yes, of course,' he murmured absentmindedly, pulling on his tie as though it was about to choke him. He was pleasant, desperately sincere and pathetically foolish—and it showed.

Lydia went back to her desk a few minutes later. The telephone rang and Steven's voice came regretfully, 'I've got a motoring case—emergency. . . could I come round for a coffee and brandy about nine? Postpone our dinner date?'

'By all means,' she said, visualising him as she spoke—tall, easy-going, with an air of blithe good humour and an obvious zest for life, his blue eyes flattering, as was his manner. Steven always put her in a lighthearted mood, and even the sound of his voice brightened any day. He flirted, but had never given her any cause for annoyance during her marriage. They met at Heath Edge, for he was included in the family friendship, and was closer to Philip than to Lance.

'I should think something to eat might be welcome, too.'

'We could still go out, of course, but I can't be sure of time.'

'There'll be sandwiches,' she compromised. ''Bye.'

Some time later, her correspondence finished, she heard the front door, heavy and imposing, close. Lance appeared in the doorway.

'Finished?' He looked at her tidy desk.

'Just this minute.' Should she tell him about Steven? They didn't usually exchange many confidences or discuss personal plans, but she said impulsively, 'Steven has an emergency. He's coming in for a brandy and coffee about nine.'

'Oh.' He said a little startlingly, 'How about slipping into the Gioconda for a drink? I could do with one. . .' He added irrelevantly, 'I wonder why human beings are so hell bent on destroying themselves, and can't deal with emotion?'

'Because there's no logic in it,' Lydia said quietly. 'Sanity flies out of the window when what's termed "love" flies in.'

'I haven't a great deal of patience with it all.' He spoke sharply. 'Or am I being pompous if I say that we've managed to behave in a civilised fashion, so why can't others?'

'Very pompous.' She stared him out. 'We weren't in love with each other, or with anyone else. All we lost was habit and familiarity. And, as you've pointed out, we were not even sexually compatible.' She got up from her desk with an air of finality. 'You may contemplate living the rest of your life in an emotionless state, but *I* certainly don't!'

Lance held her gaze, a little stupefied.

'I'm just not going to rush into a relationship,' she added. 'But I don't want the peace and calm of *not* being in love—to twist a great man's words. I want to be alive. New experiences—' She broke off a trifle awkwardly.

It wasn't what he expected. He had seen her as being content and glad to have escaped from an unsatisfactory marriage. If anything, in love with her work.

'The world your oyster, in fact?' His voice echoed strangely in the silence that followed.

'Exactly. You look surprised. . . don't tell me you're shocked?'

'You mean if you took a lover?' The words came out involuntarily, and he added firmly, 'If you cared sufficiently to take a lover, you'd care sufficiently to marry him.'

A strange thrill touched her. The word 'lover' suddenly had great potential. Perhaps that was what was missing from her life. Love in freedom; the ecstasy without ties, or promises that couldn't be kept. She gave a little laugh. 'In many ways you're quite old-fashioned, you know—'

'Old-fashioned?' His voice was gruff. 'Utter nonsense! I just happen to know a little about you, that's all.'

'Very little,' she said, her eyes meeting his, the gaze challenging. 'And I don't profess to know very much about you. Husbands and wives can be the greatest strangers of all. If we hadn't proved that, we should never have been divorced.'

He continued to look at her disarmingly, telling her, in effect, that what he had said he considered to be right, and no contradiction would alter his opinion.

She said somewhat irrelevantly, wanting to change the subject and plunging into a more contentious one, 'Clive will have returned from his holiday in Antigua and be at Heath Edge on Sunday.'

'Ah!' Lance's voice had a seal of approval. 'Clive Taylor is more your type. My father's junior partner; serious without being solemn, and thoroughly reliable.' He added with a certain satisfaction, 'I like Clive.'

'So do I,' Lydia said frankly. 'And what about *your* friends?' There was a bold calculating expression in her eyes as she spoke.

He held up both hands, palms outward, as he said firmly, 'I'm having an emotional sabbatical.'

'Even from Vivien Wayne, our glamorous physiotherapist? I noticed her at Hampstead a week or so ago.'

He frowned; a frown Lydia knew well. It was both a warning and a retreat.

'I didn't imply that I'd become a monk,' he said with infuriating evasiveness. 'How about that drink?'

She didn't hesitate. 'Thank you, but no. I want a shower and the time has already slid by. We've talked quite a bit. . . I'm duty doctor tomorrow, by the way.'

Lance looked blank and then nodded. 'Mrs Carson is off tonight.' It was a regretful sound. Mrs Carson was his housekeeper and had been with him since the divorce.

Lydia laughed. 'And if my memory serves me right, you're not at your best in the kitchen! Old-fashioned again. Modern man is quite proud of his culinary skills.'

'I'll settle for Mrs Carson and forgo the modern virtues! Make sure you get those virtues next time,' he added with a faint laugh. He opened the door for her as he spoke and they both went out into the cool spaciousness of the reception hall. She was conscious of him walking beside her and the swift, sure way in which he opened and then locked the outer door. They paused in the square, the heat striking to emphasise the coolness within the house. . . two people, each walking to their different destinations and in opposite directions. It seemed symbolic.

Steven Telford arrived at Lydia's flat soon after nine, having been delayed by a client charged with a motoring offence. He greeted her with a spontaneous friendliness, thought how attractive she looked in a blue skirt and crisp white blouse that hinted at her perfect figure and emphasized her unusually small waist. Despite the heat she looked cool. The mews flat windows were adorned by red-and-white striped canopies which kept out the glare and reduced the temperature. The bowed Georgian windows in the sitting room suggested space and gave an air of old-world charm, blending with the few antique pieces of furniture which she and Lance had each inherited from their respective grandparents. The colour scheme was dove-grey and turquoise, with touches of scarlet by way of cushions.

Steven studied her intently as he devoured the open smoked salmon sandwiches she had prepared, the salmon being a commodity she relied on for emergencies and bought from the local poulterer and fishmonger.

She found his scrutiny slightly unnerving, as though he were asking a question without resorting to words.

'Your relationships with men are rather extraordinary,' he announced somewhat startlingly.

She looked surprised, her eyebrows raised. 'Why?'

'You work with your ex-husband; you're friendly with me, and I don't think you and Clive are lovers, despite your close friendship.' He ate a sandwich composedly, his gaze still upon her while he made an assessment. 'You know I want to go to bed with you. . . The timing, somehow, has never been quite right.'

'You're not in love with me, Steven.'

'The two things are not necessarily concomitants,' he said coolly, finishing the last sandwich and lifting his brandy glass.

Lance's words tumbled over in her mind, echoing with a curious insistence. *'If you cared sufficiently to take a lover, you'd care sufficiently to marry him'.* What nonsense! she argued in ridicule. The idea made her seem suddenly prim.

'True,' she agreed, lowering her gaze.

'You have an amazing ability to suggest intimacy, while backing away from it,' he persisted.

She gave a little lilting and infectious laugh. 'You should have gone in for psychiatry instead of law!'

'So you appreciate that my judgment is sound.'

Lydia was naturally honest and she didn't dissemble. 'If that's how I appear to you, then you must have a valid point.'

'Meaning that there isn't any chemistry so far as I'm concerned—not on your side.'

'Next time, I want not only chemistry, but compatibility and *love*,' she replied.

'I'd like the moon, too,' he agreed, with scepticism.

'Emotional compromise is like an egg without salt,' she insisted.

'And you were not prepared to compromise,' he suggested, 'or you wouldn't be divorced. I must say I admire the way you and Lance have handled things. It rather fascinates me, to be honest, that any two people can be so completely indifferent to emotion after having lived together.'

'The answer being that they're probably the only people really capable of physical indifference— they've nothing more to learn about each other.'

'The chase being a greater thrill than the kill.' His eyes glowed, his interest and desire deepening.

They sat and talked until the light of evening had gone, and only the illuminations and glow of the London night sky remained.

When Steven was about to leave, he drew her into his arms, his lips parting hers, his arms suffocatingly tight about her body.

'Do I have to go?' he asked between kisses, his lips against her neck.

Lydia knew she had nothing to give except the superficial response awakened by his touch. It was an enjoyment, not an experience. Flirting was one thing; making love another. And while the phrase had been debased by flippant modern usage, she knew it still had a significance to her; that she would want to *make* love, not merely go to bed with a man.

She drew away from him gently.

'If we want to remain friends. . .' she said tentatively.

His words came sharply, 'There's no such thing as friendship between a man and a woman until they're in their dotage! Lydia—'

'I don't want a life strewn with meaningless affairs, Steven.'

'You wouldn't marry me if I asked you,' he said, a little aggrieved.

'I like you very much,' she said lightly, 'you're such a glorious philanderer. One day you'll be caught!'

'Not, obviously, by you,' he said, adding resignedly, 'Thank you for the drink and sandwiches. Now go to your virginal bed.' He added, 'I shall make a point of going to the Richmonds' on Sunday—just to see you!'

'And Vivien,' she put in. 'Our physiotherapist at Carisbrooke attracts you all!'

'You're too damned perceptive by half,' he exclaimed with a wry smile.

'That's why I'm opening the front door instead of keeping it shut,' she retorted as she saw him out.

'Coward,' he teased, as he stood on the flagstones outside the quaint, attractive house with its window-boxes glowing in the moonlight. 'But I warn you, I'm very persistent, and shall be there when you realise there's no Shangri-La.' He looked down at her seriously. 'I always win in the end.'

Lydia shivered, although the air was still warm. She didn't want to accept the words as prophetic. To have made one big mistake in her life was understandable, even excusable; two would be a disaster, and she hated failure.

Sunday morning arrived and Lydia unashamedly revelled in the luxury of idleness. Early tea taken back to bed with the newspapers; the sun streaming in through the open windows of her attractive bedroom, with its Laura Ashley prints in lilac and white and a lilac carpet that gave the tinted walls a special glow. . . London was still; its pulse no longer throbbing to the sound of traffic, the silence deeper and different from any other in the land and most welcome. She had only to shower, have her breakfast and drive the short distance to Hampstead. 'Freedom', Lance had said. 'The world your oyster'. She was enjoying the experience, and thought of Steven with indulgence, not dismissal. No woman was entirely indifferent to a man who wanted to take her to bed—provided she liked him. Lazily she discarded the papers after a while, slipped into a flimsy housecoat that matched the room, and peered down into the somnolent mews where no one stirred and cars stood in readiness for any outings. The sky was cloudless and deep blue above the rooftops, the trees in the square nearby barely moving in the soft gentle breeze. In a matter of minutes she could be in Hyde Park, with its masses of flowers, space, and escape from the city. She thought wistfully that if her parents had been alive, she would have been going to Wiltshire and Marlborough amid the beauty of the downland countryside, and Savernake Forest. It struck her with gratitude how big a gap Edward and Marion Richmond, her in-laws, had filled in her life, and that they would always be a bond between her and Lance.

Heath Edge stood back from the road skirting the Heath, giving a view over the magnificent panorama that encompassed London, like a gigantic tapestry woven in shades of green and gold, with the magic haze of blue that softened the outline and gave it, contradictorily, illimitability. The Edge, as Marion said, had never really made up its mind in which direction it intended to go, and rambled on, some rooms very large, some small; but all comfortable and welcoming, with little corridors darting about from unexpected steps. The long L-shaped sitting room was one of chintz, well-worn rugs and highly-polished woodblock floors. Most of the furniture had been handed down and had a story of happiness to tell.

Edward and Marion happened to be standing in the hall with Lance as Lydia arrived. Edward was in his mid-fifties, greying, tall, with a lean body and clean-cut sensitive features—a doctor of the old school, while Marion was a woman who thoroughly enjoyed being 'Mrs', never at any time wishing to be 'Ms', and revelled in the running of a house with the help of a 'daily', preparing huge meals for mostly ravenous males, while always ready to dance, or take off, at a moment's notice should Edward be able to sneak an unexpected break.

The summer sun touched Lydia with a sensuous warmth as she got out of the car, having parked it in the drive which was away from the practice quarters. Lance came to the front door, smart in his casual flannels, open-necked light grey shirt and multi-coloured cravat.

'Hello there!' he said, and surprisingly held out his left hand, clasping hers in a gesture of familiarity and welcome.

She returned the pressure and met his gaze, a little startled, emotion bringing her suddenly to life, almost as though she had come out of shock.

Vivien Wayne, physiotherapist with rooms at Carisbrooke, arrived at that second and exclaimed laughingly, as she quickly got out of her car, 'Divorcees, holding hands?' She was an attractive, pencil-slim twenty-five-year-old, who had a knack of wearing silk scarves to give elegance to any outfit. On this occasion she had blended a crimson and white Christian Dior with a white sleeveless linen dress. Her dark hair was smooth, her eyes a little mysterious and questioning.

Lydia felt her own attractive summery primrose and cream print was immediately nondescript. She avoided Lance's gaze and released her hand from his.

And in that moment, Vivien said to herself, 'Lance is the man I'm going to marry. He has everything I want—financial security, power, popularity. But I shouldn't tolerate his wife working with him.'

Lydia strolled to the patio which flanked the south side of the house, from which came the sound of voices enjoying their midday drinks. Clive Taylor hurried towards her from a comfortable wicker chair. 'Oh, it's good to see you again,' he said earnestly.

He was bronzed, broad-shouldered and tall, and despite his masculinity had an air of gentleness which made him an extremely good doctor, whose work Edward Richmond valued highly.

But although Lydia smiled her welcome and met his intense gaze, she was thinking of Lance. Memories flooding back—their past intimacy, the familiarity of marriage and all that it entailed, rather like a procession of recollections disturbing her nostalgically. And she knew with selfconscious embarrassment that, while there was no question of love coming into her appraisal of him, she could not deny the sudden excitement and deep sexual attraction the touch of his hand had awakened—an attraction wholly lacking during their marriage.

CHAPTER TWO

LYDIA stood there trance-like for a second before settling down, trying to overcome her emotion. At that moment Lance hurried forward, having just answered the telephone.

'I'm sorry,' he said, his manner to Clive apologetic, 'that was Bunty to say Hester isn't well. . . I'd like you to come with me,' he added, looking at Lydia.

Both Edward and Marion overheard the words, Marion's happy, carefree face clouding. Hester Gilmore was her goddaughter; Bunty, Hester's friend, housekeeper, factotum and confidante.

Vivien, feeling abandoned, stood nearby, annoyed and always irritated by the attention given to Hester.

'Let's hope,' said Clive with a brightness he was far from feeling, 'that it's something simple.' He did not underestimate their concern.

Within a matter of minutes Lance and Lydia arrived at Hester's flat, which was on the ground floor of a converted Georgian house, giving a view over Whitestone Pond where children were merrily sailing their boats. The relaxation and tranquility of the Sunday morning was endemic in the colourful scene. Hester was twenty-three and had lived there all her life, her parents having died tragically in an air crash when she was eighteen.

Bunty—Mrs March by name, and a widow who had been with the family for ten years—well-dressed, attractive and looking far younger than sixty, greeted them, obviously concerned.

'Giddy and sick,' she hastened, used to doctors and therefore not wasting words.

Hester lay propped up on several pillows in a light airy bedroom, looking fragile, ill and appealing. . . she was blind.

'Oh, Lance,' she murmured weakly as he sat down beside her and took her hand in his.

Lydia hadn't spoken, or made her presence known, when Hester added, 'So good of you to come, too, Lydia.'

Lydia was always amazed that Hester sensed more than most people actually saw. She could tell how many people there were in a room, even if they were silent.

Lance made a detailed examination, given facts of the suddenness of the attack. His expression was solemn, his manner tender and anxious.

Lydia studied Hester with a new awareness. Usually, her shining dark, sorrel-tinted hair was coiled about her head (she was expert at managing it); now it was long and falling over her shoulders, giving her a beauty that had all the depth of a painting.

Lance satisfied himself that there was no question of a gastric disorder and every other possibility chased through his mind, since the symptoms could be evidence of so many diverse complaints, including Ménière's Disease, brain stem ischaemia, even multiple sclerosis. Equally, he clung to the possibility of viral labyrinthitis.

'I don't know where I am. . . my world has gone,' Hester said simply and with a pathos she neither realized nor intended, because she had never made an affliction of her blindness.

'We'll soon get it back,' Lance promised, flashing a glance at Lydia who was now sitting on the end of the bed.

'But what *is* it?' asked Hester. 'The sickness hasn't anything to do with my stomach—'

'I'm hoping it's a viral disorder, and I'll prescribe some tablets that should clear it up. . . you're quite certain it isn't postural—nothing to do with the way you move your body or head?'

'Certain.' She gave a little sigh. 'It's like being in a spin-drier, as I imagine one.' She forced a smile that disappeared as she grasped Lance's arm in another wave of giddiness.

Lance flicked a prescription pad from his pocket. Lydia knew he would order prochlorperazine (Stemetil).

Hester's face was turned towards him in that second, giving intensity and depth to a look that lingered poignantly in silent worship. And Lydia knew with shock and amazement that Hester was in love with him.

Lance tore the prescription from the pad and Lydia held out her hand.

'I'll go down to the chemist and get the tablets,' she said immediately—the shop was a matter of minutes away in the High Street.

Hester was listening, not wanting Lance to move.

'You're so good to me, Lydia. . . Bunty—'

'I know Bunty would go,' Lydia said swiftly, 'but I can knock someone up if I'm too late!'

Hester relaxed. To her relief she heard Lance lean back against his chair. Hearing was the sight of the blind—hearing and touch—and she slid her hand along the edge of the summer duvet, hoping he would reach out and take it again, which he did—a gesture which was the last thing Lydia saw as she hurried from the room. And as she drove down the High Street, she told herself that it was she who had been blind—blind throughout her marriage, never really seeing Lance in relation to other women, while accepting everything with a casualness that now appeared almost calculated indifference.

Meanwhile Lance sat, Hester's hand clinging to his, while he looked around the attractively furnished room. Blind from birth, she knew only the names of colours, and because the sky had been described to her in childhood, she had wanted a 'blue' carpet which had been faithfully reproduced. The oval dressing table was draped with primrose satin and lace. She could *feel* the texture of satin, and trace the pattern of lace, so that both were real to her. The fragility of primroses as she outlined them had inspired the desire for their shade to be used in the furnishings, with which she had an affinity. She knew every object on the glass top, and found a sensuous appreciation in the scent of her choice, able to name it and make comparisons. The rest of the furniture was built in, the contents of the cupboards and drawers kept in meticulous order. Anyone watching her walk around the room would never dream that she was blind. She, like all blind people, refused to accept the word, and talked about 'seeing' and 'looking at' this or that object. Her fingers would travel over any face or article, and retain its image. She was an infallible judge of character and definite in her likes and dislikes.

'Lance?' she whispered, fear in her voice.

'Yes?' His voice was low and sympathetic.

'You—you. . . won't send me. . . away?'

She slid from the pillows in a wave of giddiness, her head on his shoulder.

He held her protectively.

'My darling Hester,' he said comfortably, his lips touching the top of her head, 'it wouldn't be a question of *sending* you away, but if you needed hospitalisation. . . well then, investigation would be vital.' He helped her back on the pillows and, to his relief, Lydia returned with the prescription and some water. Lance took ten milligrams and put them on Hester's tongue, holding the glass, because Hester was too giddy to have any co-ordinated movement.

The sun streamed in through the open windows, falling directly on the bed, but Hester was not affected by the glare, and loved the warmth on her face. The sun lightened her darkness without giving her any more light, in the same way that a blazing fire suggested movement and flickered in the gloom.

'You'll relax,' Lance said hopefully. 'No, these aren't sleeping tablets, but since they should make your sickness and giddiness better. . .'

'Sleep. . . would be. . .' Her voice was incapable of sustaining any firm note, sounding weak and breathless. . . 'Now you must go.' She looked towards Lydia. 'Is Clive home?'

'Yes.' Lydia felt a little thrill of pleasure at the knowledge that he was at Heath Edge.

Hester sighed and forced a smile. Bravery and determination were stamped upon her features. 'I wanted to be with you all,' she managed to insist, her voice cracking.

'I'll come back in an hour or two,' Lance promised.

Lydia stood there, suddenly feeling alien, noticing Lance's every movement which now had significance, whereas before, she would hardly have noticed his presence.

Hester's hands fluttered shakily out towards them. A lump came into Lydia's throat. Hester seemed vulnerable and alone; shut off in her dark world now that certainty of movement was denied her. Even leaving her with Bunty seemed like desertion, and yet Lydia knew that she was in no fit state to be moved to Heath Edge, unless by ambulance.

'Bless you,' she whispered. 'I. . . shall. . . be better.'

Lance and Lydia, after a word with Bunty, went out to the car, silent, divorced from their surroundings.

'Thank God for Bunty,' said Lance as they settled into their respective seats. 'It would have been hospital otherwise.' He looked emotionally drained. 'I hate it when Hester's not well; one feels helpless— brought up sharply against truth and reality. When she said, 'I've lost *my world*. . .'

'And of course, she has,' Lydia said unevenly. 'Sureness of touch, being able to sense and to feel her way. . . giddiness must be terrifying. It's bad enough when one has all one's senses—'

'Do *you* agree that it could be viral?' he shot at her.

'I hope so; not easy to make a diagnosis. I've had a few of these cases recently when people were sick if they even opened their eyes! It's all different with Hester.'

Lance gave her a sideways glance. 'You're a great help, Lydia.'

'I haven't said anything constructive.'

'But you were there,' he murmured appreciatively.

Lydia didn't want to give importance to his words, or to be so acutely conscious of him as he sat beside her in the driving seat. His masculinity seemed a challenge, the clean-cut outline of his features rea-

wakening the same sensation that had washed over
her such a short while ago, when his hand had clasped
hers. It was, she reflected, highly ironic that she
should now be sexually conscious of her ex-husband,
while having no illusions about love. Did Lance realise that Hester was in love with him? Above all, what
were his feelings for her?

Back at Heath Edge, Marion watched as Lance
and Lydia came through the front door, hearing their
news with distress and realising that no matter what
the circumstances, or their gravity, she never saw
them together without thinking how ludicrous it was
that they were divorced, or how amazing that they
could be so casually friendly and wholly detached
from the past. No rancour, bitterness, or semblance
of emotion. She herself was an extrovert, affection-
ate without mawkishness, but having a warmth that
embraced all those with whom she came in contact.
She had never been quite sure of Lance's feelings for
Hester; how deep they were, or influenced by her
blindness. There was a time, not long after the
divorce, when she had even accepted the possibility
of her goddaughter becoming her daughter-in-law.
She knew only that she would hate to lose touch with
Lydia, whose relationship with Lance would inevitably change on his remarriage.

'How is she?' Marion asked anxiously.

Lance explained, adding that if there was no
improvement, he would get Hester into hospital. The
responsibility for Bunty would be too great otherwise, and she could always accompany Hester should
it be a dire emergency.

Vivien, eating a fork luncheon which Marion
always provided on Sundays, moved to Lance's side.
He looked at her with pleasure, realising that he must

not allow his professional anxiety to be too obvious. Having explained the circumstances, he went off with her into the dining room. Clive managed to cut in before Steven could monopolise Lydia.

'I claim first rights,' he said boldly, putting his arm through Lydia's, about to lead her away.

'Hi!' called Edward, 'I haven't even got Lydia a drink, and I'm sure she could do with one!' He had heard the news about Hester and appreciated that doctors needed to unwind the more involved they were with their respective cases.

Lydia felt hot, uneasy and troubled. She wanted to escape with Clive.

'Gin and tonic,' she said with a look which Edward understood: more tonic than gin and ice. She had a silent understanding with Edward, who was more like a favourite uncle than an ex-father-in-law.

The glass given to her, she and Clive walked out into the garden which, while not large, was beautiful. A swing hammock stood in the corner of a well-manicured lawn, and rose beds clustered without formality around the smooth paths. Willow trees, seemingly fragile but tenacious in winter, fluttered in the faint warm breeze, while a massive cypress gave an impressive finish to the scene which might have been in the heart of the country instead of within a few miles of London.

Lydia sat down gratefully and sipped her drink; Clive, sensitive to her mood, allowed a few seconds to pass in silence. They put their respective drinks on the small tables nearby. Lydia sighed and said genuinely, 'It's good to have you back.'

'Does that imply you've missed me?'

Lydia felt emotion welling within her; Hester's condition had sensitised her, bringing to the surface a mood that was new and a little frightening.

'Yes,' she said honestly.

Clive's arms went around her, his lips on hers, at first gently and then with increasing fervour, and she clung to him, passion stirring as she wanted to relax in his arms and feel all the ecstasy for which she longed.

He drew back and looked down into her eyes.

'I love you,' he said tensely. 'I have done for so long.'

Lydia started. It was a new experience to hear those words, and she responded to them like someone in a desert craving for water.

'For so long?' she echoed.

'I couldn't tell you while you were married to Lance,' he murmured, 'and afterwards you were— distant, and I've known it would be useless.'

'Then,' she asked, wide-eyed, 'what's made you change your mind today?'

'Being away; separation, and just something about you—'

'Oh, Clive. . . I never even *thought*—'

'I know,' he said flatly. 'You've not only been divorced from Lance; you've been divorced from all emotion, and sensuality didn't exist.'

'One had to make adjustments,' she reminded him.

He held her gaze. 'Will you marry me? I don't want any more pretence.'

Her eyes were direct and honest as she said, 'I want, in time, to remarry, Clive; I want to be in love, *involved,* to make up for all I feel I've missed. Perhaps my idea of love is a romantic illusion, but I know only that this time I can't settle for less. You mean a tremendous lot to me—' She made a little gesture of apology for the banality of the statement. 'There's no one I'd even consider the thought of marrying, except you; but I can't tie myself yet. I feel cheated in some indefinable way, and I hate the fact that I've failed.'

Clive said hotly, 'It takes two, Lydia.'

'Lance and I never attempted to apportion blame.'

'I wish you had.' The outburst surprised her. 'I don't understand this civilised friendship. . . Lydia—'

The sound of voices coming from the patio alerted them, and they picked up their drinks, knowing they would be observed by anyone leaving the rose arbour.

Lance and Vivien appeared, Vivien saying, 'No prizes for guessing where you were!'

Lydia raised her gaze to Lance, aware of his air of ease and yet possessiveness where Vivien was concerned, as he guided her to a deck chair, one of several that were dotted around the hammock to offer sanctuary to those who wanted to enjoy the summer sun.

'You haven't eaten,' Lance commented, addressing Lydia. He looked from face to face, conscious of the atmosphere and a certain tension.

'I'm having my meal out of this glass,' Lydia retorted.

'Not what the doctor ordered,' remarked Lance.

'But the way to keep slim,' Vivien suggested with a little laugh.

Steven sauntered towards them, missing Hester who always 'mixed' and completed the picture, enjoying Edward's geniality and Marion's cheerful welcome, to say nothing of her Cordon Bleu cooking. He assessed the emotional set-up: Clive and Lydia, Lance and Vivien. Without Hester the division was clear-cut.

'I think,' he said a little later, glancing around him, 'it's time we left.'

Clive got to his feet. 'I've a terminal case to see at the Middlesex,' he said honestly, while nevertheless resenting Steven's dictatorial manner. He was jealous of Steven and didn't try to deceive himself. He looked at Lydia. 'I'll be in touch,' he said deliberately.

Vivien gave Lance a rather beguiling smile. 'I've some notes to tackle. . . see you tomorrow.' They had already agreed to meet.

Eventually only the family was left, and they settled on the patio like people talking with a sick relative lying ill upstairs. The house had taken to itself a quietness that shut out even the hum of insect life and gave the illusion that the curtains had been drawn so that the windows were in shadow.

'If there's no improvement I shall send her into St Matthew's. I've already been in touch.' Lance spoke as though they were already talking of Hester and that it was superfluous to mention her name.

But after another visit and telephone call, he said finally, 'Come with me, Lydia. . . if she's asleep, all well and good—for tonight, at least. If not, you'll be moral support for Bunty in any case.'

Lydia noticed that he assumed she hadn't any appointments. She drove in her own car.

But Hester was still asleep and had a Madonna-like look as she lay against the pillows, almost upright, her small hands lying over the blue and primrose duvet, curled up like a child's.

Lance, Lydia and Bunty exchanged glances and tiptoed from the room.

'She didn't have any sleep last night—or hardly any,' said Bunty. 'She wouldn't have you disturbed until she was really frightened and expected for lunch.' She sighed and put her hands out helplessly.

'And when Hester makes up her mind, there's nothing I can do; her hearing is so acute that there's no possibility of my making any secret telephone call.'

'We must do something about that,' Lance said meaningly. 'Put an instrument in your bedroom.'

'We've got one in the hall, sitting room and Hester's bedroom,' Bunty reminded him, and the semblance of a smile touched her lips for the first time.

He nodded. 'We'll see.' Which meant he'd have his own way. 'I'll come back later on—about nine-thirty.' He handed her a telephone number. 'If you want me I'm there, on your doorstep. Lydia hasn't eaten since breakfast and I'm going to take her out for a meal at La Bella Rosa.'

Lydia stared at him. He was talking *for* her, as did so many husbands and wives without even realising it. She just gave Bunty a look of assent.

Hester heard the murmur of voices through a series of sensations, rather like coming out of an anaesthetic. The dark space that was her world was no longer spinning full circle, but rhythmically rocking, her heartbeat echoing in her body. She had lost the violence of being precipitated into nothingness.

They thought she was still asleep. . . La Bella Rosa, the resturant favoured by the family and to which Lance and Lydia had always gone. . . it was very near. 'I'm not sick any more,' she thought disjointedly, 'just unreal. . . What time is it? Not black like night. . . but of *course,* it's evening, or they wouldn't be going out to dinner.' Lance had said he'd come back later on and she could hear him still whispering. She wouldn't disturb them now; they'd stay with her otherwise, and she'd already spoilt their day. She thought in silent gratitude, *'Oh God, thank you for helping me to be a little better. . . thank you. . .'*

The sun was still warm. . . Lance; he must never know that she loved him; she must always behave like the trusting friend whom he protected because she couldn't see. His hand had held hers so lovingly in the torment of her giddiness. . . If I move, he and Lydia will come back. . . breathe deeply. . . help them by trying to sleep again. Ah, the front door was opening, the sudden gentle breeze from outside mingling with the air from her own open windows, stirring the curtains. The blind hadn't a sixth sense, as was generally supposed, but were so attuned to sound and movement that it seemed they must possess one.

The front door was shut and Bunty was coming along the corridor, tiptoeing. It would be good for her to have a little time to relax, and she probably hadn't had anything to eat. There was a slight stir at the door and Hester could 'see' her looking in to satisfy herself that all was well. She could even hear that little catch of breath in thankfulness. . . In that moment Hester was drawn back into a blissful world of dreams.

Lance and Lydia went into the coolness of La Bella Rosa, with its marble floors and tiny waterfalls—climbing plants decorating shaded green walls. Wine racks formed a backcloth against an attractive small bar which was illuminated by multi-coloured lights. The tablecloths and napery were a pale amber, and a delicate vase of summer flowers decorated each table.

Lance and Lydia were at home there, and Giuseppe welcomed them as he had done before, during, and after their marriage. He and his wife ran the family business to which his son and daughter gave their loyalty and expertise.

'Nothing fancy, Giuseppe; we've got a sick patient, so I may be called,' said Lance as they sat down rather wearily at the table, never too optimistic to believe the crisis was really over.

Giuseppe, a round-faced, bright-eyed, attractive Italian, pursed his lips, shook his head and said, 'I'm sorry. . . Cold or hot, doctor?'

'One of your salmon dishes for me,' said Lydia. 'I couldn't face meat.'

'Make that two,' said Lance, 'and how about a glass of white wine?'

'One glass?' came the attractive accented voice. 'I get you something special. Leave it to me.'

Lance said, when they were alone, 'It's a good idea to have a meal here. And I'm glad we insisted that Edward and Marion go to the Festival Hall as they'd arranged.'

'I agree.' Lydia spoke quietly. 'I don't think there'll be any complications, and we can relax for a short while.'

He looked around him, then somewhat intently back to her. 'This corner table seems to have been monopolised by the family, and although the place is nearly full, we're apart somehow. Strange, we've eaten here through every sort of crisis, yet still return!'

'That's the reward for being civilised.' She didn't want to notice his tan, or the casual smartness of his clothes. His physical appeal cut across the natural friendliness.

His expression was reflective. 'One could be in danger of confusing that word with indifference. It's so easy to be reasonable when one isn't involved emotionally. Perhaps ex-husbands and wives are the only people who can appreciate that.'

'Meaning that pleasant indifference is our bond,' she countered.

His faint smile was intriguing.

'I wouldn't go as far as that.' He shook his head. 'We can't hurt each other any more. That simplifies everything.'

Lydia lowered her gaze. She didn't want to be his wife; she didn't want any involvement, and yet, at that second, quite irrationally, she would like him to be able to kiss her—not with remembrance, or nostalgia, but with sensuality.

Their meal was served, the wine drunk slowly, the conversation easy and very much concerned with professional matters. It was when they were drinking their coffee that she said involuntarily. 'Clive has asked me to marry him.'

She watched Lance closely, waiting for his reaction.

His reply was smooth and disarming. 'I told you I thought he was right for you. I presume you said no.'

Emotion stirred. 'Why assume that?'

'Because otherwise you would have said, "I'm going to marry Clive". I don't have to be Sherlock Holmes to work that out.'

They didn't laugh, just looked at each other speculatively.

'Two failed marriages would be intolerable,' Lydia said, and sighed.

Lance held her gaze intently.

'We should, by rights, make ideal second marriages, Lydia. We've come through all this remarkably well.' His smile was broad and infectious. 'Nothing like self-congratulation! We've learned the value of friendship and cut out all the dead wood.'

Lydia felt strangely insecure, glad of Lance's approval and yet cautiously retreating, regretting having been honest about the proposal. It seemed rather childish to confide in him.

Their gaze held and then lowered.

'Hester,' he said, his voice subdued. 'I'd like to get back to her.'

There was something very personal in his attitude, seeming to emphasise that this interlude had merely served a purpose while they waited and caught up on a necessary meal.

Hester was awake on their return. She looked very pale and her dark, pansy-like sightless eyes seemed to have sunk a little in her oval face.

'Not nearly so giddy.' Her voice hadn't any strength in it, and although she made every effort, it was thin and shaky. 'And I've. . . spoilt. . . your day—Sunday, too. . . I must look terrible.' She forced a smile.

'Your skin is like satin,' Lydia said encouragingly and truthfully.

'Doesn't. . . feel like it.' Hester indicated the dressing table. 'Not like the satin there.'

'Your fingers are too critical,' Lance said softly.

Hester put one hand over the other in a stroking movement. They were her eyes, and she was unconsciously emphasising the fact—a gesture which made tears gush to Lydia's eyes.

'I want you to stay in bed,' Lance said firmly, 'until I see you tomorrow. Just go to the bathroom, that's all. There are no miracle cures, and you need rest.'

Hester sighed.

'I've a lot of typing to do,' she explained in a rush. She could touch-type perfectly, and having been taught Braille, did a great deal of charitable work for the blind, since her parents had left her well provided for.

'When I say so,' Lance ordered, 'not before. I know you: if you feel even half human, you'll be up on the Heath!' His words held secret admiration as well as astonishment.

'I won't fight,' she promised.

Bunty was reassuring as Lance and Lydia were leaving. 'She's going to be all right, I know it.'

'Bless you, Bunty,' Lydia said in a tone that Lance seconded with a nod.

He and Lydia went out into the sapphire blue summer night. Whitestone Pond glistened like a lake in the moonlight. The Heath swept illimitably and magnificently into the distance, the lights of London hanging in the soft mists that lay upon the city.

'Thank you for giving up all of today,' said Lance as they sauntered to their respective cars. 'I don't usually want someone to hold my hand, but Hester's different, and I value your opinion.' He stared ahead and then looked up at the moon which emerged from a bank of cloud, imperious, majestic.

Lydia was trembling.

And suddenly he leaned forward and brushed her cheek, his touch thrilling her with a new excitement, making her long to turn her lips to his. For one ecstatic moment she thought he was going to put his arms around her, but with a sudden swift movement he drew back.

'Thank you again. . . Goodnight, Lydia.'

He stood and watched her drive away.

CHAPTER THREE

IT was at the end of the family planning session the following Friday afternoon when Mrs Trent reminded Lydia that Mrs Alma Craig had a late appointment.

'Ah, yes,' Lydia remembered.

Alma Craig was thirty-seven, had a daughter of fifteen and a half and a son of fourteen, but as she sat opposite Lydia in the patients' chair, she could have passed for someone in her late twenties. Her fair hair was loose and shaped about her head; she had a clear tanned skin and deep blue eyes, that were now unsmiling.

'Trouble?' Lydia prompted.

'Yes.' The word came on a sigh. 'It's about Odile.'

'Your daughter.' Lydia groaned inwardly; the word 'pregnant' was never far away from her judgments. She knew Odile, who looked eighteen and was advanced for her years.

As though following Lydia's trend of thought, Mrs Craig hastened, 'It's a question of contraception.' She shook her head and made a little helpless gesture. 'I agree with her consulting you. . . what can one *do* when one really comes up against these problems? She isn't sixteen yet, and the whole thing seems fantastic. She makes me feel like her grandmother when I try to reason with her. It isn't as though she's been brought up in a narrow restricted atmosphere. You can't live in a modern world with blinkers on, and

47

she and I have been—well, more like sisters.'

'Or you wouldn't be talking like this now,' Lydia remarked.

'It's the narrow margin between discipline and licence—'

Lydia watched the knuckles of Alma Craig's hands whiten, the tension mount.

'She has a boy-friend, I take it?'

'No one special; she's got in with the wrong set, where everyone follows the lead of everyone else. Odile wants to be prepared for any eventuality and tacitly suggests that if intercourse is part of the scene. . . I'm not *old,* Dr Richmond, but I'm out of my depth. I can't physically stop her doing anything she pleases, and I didn't want, or expect, her to be a little girl in a party dress. I hoped that we'd instilled a healthy attitude towards sex and that she might eventually want to get married—' she paused, 'no doubt after having lived with her boy-friend or fiancé. . . but this possibility of promiscuity under age. . . all the hazards, the risks. A pregnant fifteen-year-old—these are the facts,' she exclaimed, her voice shaking.

'And you want me to prescribe contraceptives?'

'Not "want", Dr Richmond, but I prefer she comes to you through the front door. I mustn't lose her confidence and trust. There may be things she can tell you that she can't, or won't, tell me. I'm not in a position to judge whether you would have thought she was a subject for the pill, or whether I should be consulted. It's very much in the doctor's hands these days. All I know is that she's defiant, secretive in many ways, and difficult about life generally.'

'It's *something* that she wanted *you* to see me. Not usual; and a step in the right direction.'

'Precautionary and a concession, although she's in a highly emotional state. One has to choose one's words with care.' Mrs Craig shook her hair back with an attractive little gesture, looking very young and vulnerable. 'Some of these people are on drugs, and one faces the next step with horror.' Her voice strengthened. 'You can't fall back on the philosophy that it won't happen to your child. These are all someone's children.'

Lydia suggested, 'There could be a great deal of bravado in her defiance, you know.'

'Which reinforces my belief that you're far more likely to deal with her wisely than I am.' She met Lydia's gaze unflinchingly. 'This must be a familiar scene to you.' She made a little expressive gesture. 'I am, I admit, out of my depth, as I've already said. I thought I was so modern and could deal with anything, but when it comes to it I'm not trendy after all. They don't take into account even the legality of their behaviour, being under age. . . she's ready to face any challenge at the moment.'

'It's a great help to be put in the picture by the parent,' Lydia said appreciatively.

'And such a relief to be able to *talk*. . . I don't even know if she's afraid she's pregnant.' The blue eyes clouded, regret and sadness haunted her voice as she added, 'We've been such a happy, carefree family.'

Lydia had known them for the past six months and always pigeonholed them as 'that nice Craig family.'

'How about your son Tom?' she asked hopefully, to lighten the gloom.

The ghost of a smile came to Alma Craig's face. 'Oh, he's well into computers, working out programmes, software, and all the rest of it. With Gerald (her husband) a computer engineer, I should have one of the first robots to do the chores—' She broke off painfully. 'I can't believe that all this is happening with Odile. It comes over me like some nightmare.'

'I'd like to see her as soon as possible.' Lydia switched through to Mrs Trent and arranged an appointment for the following Tuesday at five.

'She can come straight from school,' Alma Craig said. The incongruousness of it struck them both, and was expressed in the look they exchanged. 'I must be a square, after all,' came the husky comment.

'That's a virus from which all parents suffer,' Lydia assured her consolingly, 'no matter what their age-group!'

Alma Craig left. She was at breaking point.

Lance joined Lydia in her room at the end of the day. His gaze was perceptive as he said, 'Problems?'

She outlined the Craig case, the fear, bewilderment, apprehension and sadness on Alma Craig's young face filling her with compassion.

'Some teenagers terrify me,' he said frankly. 'You're confronted with a schoolgirl with a maths book in one hand, and the latest on contraception and sex in the other.' He paused and abridged that, 'Yet, reversing the coin, we've never had a better crowd to deal with. Oh, they're probably living with their boy-friend or fiancé, but they're ambitious, hard-working, well-travelled and often Cordon Bleu cooks! The juxtaposition is amazing. And they're mostly involved in some good cause. Whether or not one agrees with their particular views is immaterial.'

'I'm afraid Odile Craig is in the former category and a very different proposition.'

Lance looked at Lydia intently, transferring his authority in a warning expression. 'Don't forget that you're in command, and the half-child, half-woman characters are all aware of your position. They know that "the doctor" has the final say. No matter how intractable they may be, they're not lacking in self-preservation when it comes to it.'

'You're very reassuring.'

The professional mood slipped away from her in that moment and she remembered his farewell the previous Sunday, having told herself she would not dwell on the folly of physical attraction, aware of its pitfalls. She wondered if she could, with impunity, suggest that they have a drink together that evening. Hester was, while not wholly recovered, well on the way to being back to normal, so didn't present any problem.

Lance stood at the windows overlooking the tree-lined square.

'There's something seductive about a summer evening,' he mused. 'It offers so much that's tempting.'

A knock came at the door and they looked at each other in surprise and impatience. The staff had gone; the house was quiet and empty and they were enjoying those moments.

Vivien stood there, striking in an austerely simple white linen dress. She beamed at Lance.

'I tried your room,' she said frankly, and gave a teasing laugh.

Lydia felt a wave of disappointment; the intrusion couldn't have been more ill-timed from her point of view. Lance's remarks had offered a perfect prelude for her suggestion of a drink.

Lance smiled. 'Lydia and I mostly congratulate, or console, each other at the end of the day.'

'You're an amazing couple,' Vivien said blatantly. She was watching them intently, her thoughts racing.

Lydia felt the colour rising in her cheeks, but she managed to counter, 'Nothing like work as a basis for sanity.'

'Implying that most divorced people aren't sane?' Vivien gave a little doubtful laugh. 'I'm sure I couldn't be friendly with an ex-husband. . . I'm not placid enough.'

Resentful emotion made Lydia angry. The remark seemed denigrating, and she was aware that Lance was watching Vivien intently, seeming to be summing her up, possibly making new discoveries. She had deliberately come into the picture during recent weeks, insinuating herself at Heath Edge and taking advantage of Steven's association with the family. For a reason Lydia could not define, she shrank from the increasing familiarity, seeing it almost as a threat. She had nothing against Vivien, but she was not her type and she knew that the last thing she wanted was for Lance to become too friendly with her. The suggestion of jealousy was ludicrous, she insisted. Yet in fairness, she argued, why shouldn't Vivien want to attract him? Women had always found him fascinating. Also he was a free man and possibly all the more intriguing because of the past.

The telephone rang on Lydia's private line and she said, 'Ah, hello, Clive.'

'Any hope of dinner tonight?'

Lydia didn't hesitate and said with enthusiasm, 'Yes; I'd like that.'

'I'll pick you up at seven-thirty.' He sounded delighted.

Lance said to Vivien, when Lydia had replaced the receiver, 'Since I'm on call, how about your coming and having a meal with me at the flat? Mrs Carson is always prepared for someone extra.'

Vivien hesitated long enough for there to be an element of suspense, then said lightly, 'Thank you.'

'Or we could go for a meal locally. So long as Mrs Carson has my telephone number.'

'The flat would be peaceful.' Vivien added, 'As we all live around here there are no driving problems—or drinking. It's a very convenient area, with Hyde Park a matter of a few minutes away, to say nothing of all the restaurants. Park Lane on our doorstep, too, if we should want hotels.' She finished hurriedly, 'Now I must dash! We physiotherapists also work, you know—paperwork, too, after hours.'

'Sevenish,' said Lance, referring to the meal.

'A bit early.' She didn't want to be too eager.

'Suit yourself; I usually eat about eight, but there are no hard and fast rules.'

Vivien crossed to the door and paused. 'Oh, by the way, I've kept in touch with Hester and we're going out into the country when she's really better. I know Bunty drives her everywhere, but this will be a change.'

Both Lance and Lydia looked surprised. Vivien had not previously appeared to show any particular interest in Hester.

'Oh, good,' Lance exclaimed, pleased. 'She'll enjoy your company. I warn you, she can tire you out if you go for a walk.'

Vivien smiled indulgently.

'She's still denied a great deal,' she said gently, as she shut the door behind her.

Lance said thoughtfully, 'You know, Lydia, it's very easy to misjudge a girl like Vivien. She's so elegant and poised that one is apt to overlook the more human side. I've been inclined to think of her as hard. Shows how wrong one can be.'

Lydia met his gaze. She didn't speak.

The atmosphere tensed as he said a trifle critically, 'You're not particularly fond of her, are you?'

She answered edgily, 'I've rather shared your opinion.'

'Touché! A few faults don't make a woman, or a man, any the less attractive. We're not liked because of our virtues. In fact, they're rarely taken into account when things go wrong. We have evidence of that. . .'

They were studying each other warily. His words about the summer evening echoed tantalisingly. As she stood there, the past rushed up at her and she heard herself repeating the words at that final scene before they agreed to divorce. *'We can't go on living together.'* She had spoken with a calm that hid her distress, remembering how, even then, she had been aware of what might be termed Lance's arrogant good looks and the expression in his eyes as they had narrowed, their dark intensity secretive and disarming.

He, too, was remembering, and their expression changed to a questioning, baffled consternation, as though they were suddenly ensnared by a nostalgia neither wished to dwell upon. He moved out of range and, again, looked out of the window. The room seemed hot and airless, and Lydia said abruptly, 'I must get back to change . . . Would you like me to take the calls after I get home? Give you a ring?'

He swung back; their gaze met.

'No, thanks all the same. You'll probably be late, and anyway, you're entitled to your evening.'

She murmured her thanks.

He strode to the door, and hesitated, his voice was low, 'Don't get married again too soon. . . I'm in no mood for change at the moment!'

'That cuts both ways,' she flashed back.

'Huh!' he mocked the possibility, and went out. The door opened again in a split second. 'I'm going to have a look at Mrs Brampton. She's due tomorrow.'

'Oh, yes,' Lydia exclaimed. She knew the Bramptons. This was their second child. They wanted a son, and a scan had confirmed that they'd get their wish. 'He fusses,' she added. 'Good idea to go along before he continually rings you to tell you she's started. Is the nurse there?'

'Due this afternoon. Another thing I want to check on; she was supposed to come a few days ago, but her last case was late and her schedule was put out. I know it's pleasant to have the offspring at home, but there isn't the trauma in hospital!'

'You're very involved with the baby cases.' The remark came involuntarily.

Their eyes met, the look lingering and then falling away. They had decided not to have a family for three years. . . Lydia wondered what would have happened had that plan gone wrong. Would they have divorced if a child had been involved? It struck her that she was forever asking questions to which there were no answers.

Lydia saw Clive with a little thrill of pleasure as he stood at the front door later that evening. He had come from hospital where, earlier, he had attended a salpingo oophorectomy—surgical removal of the ovary and fallopian tubes—and was checking up on the patient's progress. The faint smell of ether hung about him and he looked attractive in his lightweight grey suit. She wanted to fall in love with him, or even to risk agreeing to marry him, in that moment of foolish contemplation. As it was she just said, 'Clive,' and gave him a welcoming smile.

He admired her white lace blouse and black silk skirt, and said so. He had a gentle charm that was reassuring, and Lydia knew he appealed to her more than any other man of her acquaintance; she felt a sense of pride in the fact that he wanted to marry her.

'Unless you had somewhere special in mind,' she suggested, 'why don't we walk around to Martinique?'

'I'd thought of the Club,' he said. It was in St James' and he, Edward and Lance belonged to it. The Creswell Club overlooked the Park, and had the old-fashioned elegance of large chandeliered rooms, a massive staircase and all the niceties too often discarded today. Lydia liked it, and family occasions were always celebrated there. They were well known, and Edward was a life member, as was his father before him. 'But Martinique would mean that I could leave the car here—a good idea.'

Lydia picked up her handbag from the small bookcase in the lobby, shut and locked the door, and they began the few minutes' walk to Connaught Village. In the near distance Hyde Park looked cool and green; the rush hour was over, the streets empty. It was an oasis by comparison with its surroundings.

Martinique was small, artistic; the décor blue and gold, with rich velvet hangings and a small bar with wine racks framing it. It specialised in fish and its seafood was excellent. They chose lobster and half a bottle of champagne, since Clive had to drive after the meal.

'A convenient drink, champagne,' Clive said with a smile. 'You can serve it for any purpose and at any time of day, including breakfast.' He changed his attitude as he said, 'I've visualised this when I was away—our having dinner together. There's so much I want to say, Lydia. Will you bear with me if I ask a few personal questions?'

'I'll try.' She felt nervous.

He waited until the lobster was served, the glasses filled, before he asked, 'Is it your intention to go on working with Lance for much longer?'

It wasn't what she had expected, and she said on a note of surprise, 'It isn't a long-term project. I've already told him I shall be moving on before long . . .' She held his gaze. 'Why do you ask?'

'Because if you married me, I couldn't stand the situation. I find it hard enough now.'

She looked startled. 'But it's been such a convenient arrangement, from which we've both benefited. Lance losing his partner so tragically and my being temporarily at a loose end. . . I think I'd like to have a trip on a liner—get a job and see a little of the world at the same time.' She stopped, realising that the remark dismayed him.

'That doesn't seem to leave much room for me,' he said heavily.

Lydia looked down into her glass. 'I haven't had much time to get used to the idea of your wanting to marry me, Clive. Marriage hasn't been on the agenda.' As she spoke she recalled what she had said to Steven about her desires for the future, and his reply, *'I'd like the moon, too'.*

'I can appreciate that, but will you now put it firmly on the agenda and give it top priority? I'm not the most patient of men and I couldn't live in anyone else's shadow,' he added firmly.

She looked surprised.

'Meaning Lance?'

'He *was* your husband. Reverse the situation and imagine how you would feel if you were in love with me.'

Lydia sighed. 'Put like that—' A little uncomfortable sensation gripped her. She didn't want to bring Lance into it, or remember the sensual overtones that had recently disturbed her, the more so since she was not involved with him in any other way. It made her feel slightly ridiculous and was a complete contradiction of everything they professed and had lived up to. She told herself that physical attraction was a mirage that led only to disillusionment and self-ridicule.

She said, a little breathless, 'Quite honestly, Clive, even seeing your point of view doesn't alter the facts. Lance and I are good friends; two adjusted people, if you like. I should, as I've said, be moving on. We're both almost certain to marry again; it would be ridiculous to assume otherwise. All this makes him seem suddenly important—an issue.'

'God forbid! I like him; we're friends. In fact it's all too damned friendly,' he added crisply. 'I'm never allowed to forget for a moment that you've been his wife.'

She shook her head. 'I'm afraid there's nothing you can do about that. To dwell on it is sheer folly.'

He sighed. 'You're so calm about it all!'

'That should reassure you.' She gave a little laugh. 'I didn't realise we were coming out to talk about my ex-husband! If it will make you any happier, he's with Vivien. She's at the flat having dinner with him.'

Clive put a hand across the table.

'I'm sorry,' he said apologetically. 'Forgive me.'

Lydia let her hand remain in his for a second and held his gaze. 'I want to be in love with you, Clive.

You're so right; everything would be ideal. But I can't pretend. I'm not in love with anyone. Why can't we have control over our emotions? It's so infuriating!'

He exclaimed, his voice deepening, 'I'm willing to risk marrying, *knowing* you don't love me . . .'

'Oh, Clive! You don't realise what you're saying. Words are so easy to utter and so hard to live up to—
' 'But don't you see? You don't want to live a celibate life; drifting, waiting, if you like, to fall in love as though you were having a crush on a film star? Just think. . . you could come into the practice. Edward and I need help—' His enthusiasm grew as he gave utterance to the words and the picture built up.

Lydia shivered; it was too tempting for her to rule out. She would never find a man she admired more than Clive; she was not physically unmoved by him and their understanding of each other had always been great. There was no question of her remaining much longer with Lance; the flaws would inevitably begin to reveal themselves and if he and Vivien—or, she thought, and paused almost with shock—he and Hester should marry, then the severance would come anyway. Lance was inscrutable where his emotions were concerned and his protective devotion to Hester, his enjoyment of her company, had always been a factor to reckon with, but his feelings were never a subject for discussion.

'You're rushing ahead,' she said with faint desperation.

'I intend to,' Clive persisted. 'I own the Hampstead house which you've always liked. No problem there.'

She agreed. Disposing of her flat would be simple, but a little tremor of apprehension went over her: she would hate to give it up. In fact when it came to it, she did not want to be precipitated into upheaval.

Perversely, she thought, Clive would have been more attractive to her had he not told her of his love; suspense sharpening anticipation. And even as she dwelt on the observation, she told herself she was behaving like a romantic adolescent. In truth her failed marriage had emphasised the mental and physical denial of an unsatisfactory relationship. She felt cheated. Yet the picture Clive painted would appear to embrace perfection.

'You've thought of everything,' she exclaimed reflectively. 'I must say I can see myself working with you and Edward. It wasn't practical to be more than a locum to Lance. . . I notice you expect me to go on working,' she added teasingly.

He exclaimed, 'Good heavens, only if you want to. It never occurred to me that you'd consider giving up.'

'Quite right—I'd hate to.' Her heart quickened its beat. 'And any children wouldn't be a problem.' She spoke naturally.

They looked at each other in understanding.

'I was afraid Steven might be a rival,' Clive admitted.

She shook her head. 'I like Steven; he's good fun to flirt with on occasion, but not to take seriously. He doesn't even take himself seriously, so one knows the score.'

'That's a relief, anyway. I'm beginning to feel a little more confident.' He added, 'Plenty of people fall in love after marriage, Lydia. Couldn't you—?'

'Don't rush me,' she begged on a pleading note. 'Remember, I've failed once. The responsibility a second time seems so much greater.'

They finished their meal and walked back to the flat. London was illuminated against a backcloth of the afterglow which threw rainbow colours across the brilliantly lit buildings, picking them out, vast and impressive.

'Thank you for this evening,' she said gently as they reached the mews and paused beside the car.

He looked down at her.

'I love you, Lydia, and I'll try to be patient.'

She gave him a little wistful smile, her pulse quickening. But he didn't kiss her; just said goodnight and wisely drove away.

The telephone rang just as she reached the sitting room and she heard Hester say, 'I've just been talking to Marion. . . I'm going to stay for a week!' There was excitement in her voice. 'Bunty will be able to visit her sister—not that she couldn't do that if I were here, but it will fit in so well.' She hurried on, 'Will you be able to come over as often?'

'I'll stay the weekend after this,' Lydia promised. 'We can celebrate. I haven't forgotten it will be your birthday.' She added swiftly, 'And you're still feeling better?'

'Much. I went for a walk this afternoon, all along by the Heath. It was beautiful—the air and the scent of the trees.'

Hester had been trained by a mobility officer to use the long cane, which was a combined buffer and scanner to detect obstacles two paces ahead, so that she could deal with the hazards of trees, lamp-posts, parked cars. She could also detect steps, kerbs and holes in the pavement. To Lydia it was miraculous how Hester went about as though sighted. She had been taught to estimate distance and direction by the use of sounds: how to walk in a straight line by moving parallel to the traffic on the roads. Her hearing was so acute that she could detect large objects by echolocation.

'June is a beautiful month,' Lydia said.

'I think every month bring its special message.'

The only thing Lydia had particularly to remember when dealing with Hester was never to assume she could not do things for herself. Her independence atoned for the handicap, but her venturesome spirit sometimes nearly gave Bunty a heart attack.

'I spoke to Lance a little earlier,' said Hester, a trifle hurriedly. 'Vivien was with him. I spoke to her, too. She and I are going out into the country one day. . . I mustn't keep you, it's late; but I love the June nights when the sun has gone down and the flowers smell so *fresh*. Goodnight, Lydia. I'm so glad to be going to Edward and Marion. They're such *fun!*'

Hester replaced the receiver and sat by the open window in the sitting room, the breeze fanning her face and the echo of voices from the few passers-by bringing the scene to life. It was not darkness to her, but a world conjured out of learning and imagination. The sound of laughter stimulating happiness, or the cry of a child, distress. Everything was highly sensitised and she was attuned to all moods, both of people and nature.

Bunty came in, accustomed to the lack of lighting in the room, and switched on the desk lamp, which made Hester say, 'I always forget to do that. One of these days I shall have you falling over!' Hester never fell over; she knew every object in the various rooms and provided they were kept in their customary places she could walk steadily and unhesitatingly.

'Shall we have a cup of tea?' Hester suggested. 'I'll get it.'

Bunty didn't protest. Hester had all the gadgets available, among them a tea dispenser which gave a measured quantity at a time, with a small electronic device placed on the side of the cup with a pair of wires going down to the bowl. When the liquid was poured in the cup, and touched the wires, a noise was made. There were two sets of wires, one to judge the quantity of milk, the other to indicate when the cup was almost full. Bunty often wondered if Hester's particular love of tea was not bound up with the independence it gave her to make it. Her capacity for work in the kitchen never failed to amaze Bunty, used though she was to watching Hester's expertise. Many of the implements were explained in Braille and there was a clock with hands beneath the glass and over it, so that the time could be told by touch.

When the tea was made and brought in on a tray, Hester sat down and said with a little smile of happiness, 'Lance is going to take me to La Bella Rosa next week. I love that—the cool marble and the sound of the fountains. I can imagine myself in Italy. I've read a lot about it and one gets the mood and the feeling of warmth, and how happy and close the family life is.' She looked thoughtful. 'They don't put their old people in homes like we do here. . . I think so much about people. I'm so very lucky, Bunty. I have everything to help me, and you—above all, you. I know I can't do *everything* alone, and you make it all so easy. When we go shopping and I can't see the prices, you never get impatient. Once I can *feel* the things. . .' She went on disjointedly, 'Vivien sounded very kind—different, somehow, when she spoke to me earlier and suggested our going out. I've rather thought that she found me a—a—well, a bore. Oh, I can understand it!'

'*Bore?*' Bunty's voice held disgust. 'That's the last thing!' Actually, Bunty regarded Vivien with reservation and wondered why she had suddenly suggested taking Hester out.

Hester went on, 'It's a question that some people don't make you feel apart. They accept you as you are, and allow you to do everything possible for yourself. It's when people talk to you as though you're helpless, or not there, that it hurts. But there's so much kindness. And when I'm out and it's a very busy road, some people are so gentle when they help me across the road, but others who are nervous and a little frightened hold on to me as though I'll blow away. I can visualise each one and am grateful to them. . .' A wistful expression gave her a poignant appeal. 'Bunty, I—I can say anything to you, can't I?' The words were tentative.

'Of course.'

'Do you—' there was a faintly shy pause, 'do you think I shall ever marry?'

Bunty felt that all the air had been drained from the room.

'If you find a man you could love, of course. But you're a very particular young lady.' Bunty deliberately forced a light note into her voice, knowing where Hester's affections lay and that even as she asked the question, she had Lance in mind.

'He might not love me,' came the quiet observation, followed by a gentle admission, 'I would like to be loved; it would make me—' she paused, trying to find the right word and finally adding, 'it would make me feel *whole*.'

Tears stung Bunty's eyes. She said slowly and with a deep truth, 'When you marry, you will be loved very deeply—'

'I wouldn't want to be a burden, or—or hamper anyone, but I'm not helpless and I could do quite a bit—proper work, I mean.' Hester paused again and then rushed on, following her own trend of thought, 'People—peoplelike Lance, for instance, always need receptionists, but I'm being silly. . . we never know what's going to happen tomorrow. I told you Lance was going to take me to La Bella Rosa, didn't I?'

Bunty said, 'Yes. . . I'm going to have an early night.' She thought it wise not to prolong the conversation about Lance, but an uneasiness stirred within. Hester was so vulnerable; it would be very easy for anyone, she thought, to hurt her unwittingly.

And as though on the same wavelength, and just before seeing Odile Craig the following Tuesday, Lydia said to Lance, 'I hear you're taking Hester to La Bella Rosa on Thursday.'

He was sitting at his desk, signing the last letter, and jerked his head up, speaking sharply as he demanded,

'Do I detect a note of disapproval in your voice?'

CHAPTER FOUR

LIDYIA shrank from the harshness of Lance's tone. It was foreign to their present relationship. Nevertheless she knew that his assessment was correct, but it was based on the wrong assumption. She had no wish to interfere with his friendships, but she was protective where Hester was concerned and at a disadvantage because she knew that Hester was in love with him.

She said quickly, 'It's not for me to have any reactions and certainly not to interfere in your affairs, personal or otherwise.'

'But there's something at the back of your mind,' he persisted. 'Give me credit for knowing a little about you. I appreciate your honesty, since we both realise your attitude isn't based on any jealousy.'

She met his gaze very levelly, knowing she could not escape explanation.

She dared to say, 'It's very easy for a man to convey more than he actually feels.' Unnerved by his stillness, she hurried on, 'And Hester's position makes her very vulnerable.'

There was a heavy silence, but no protest. Lance didn't avoid her gaze; if anything he held it a little longer than was necessary before saying, 'You're a very perceptive person.'

Did that mean, she asked herself, that he was tentatively admitting to being emotionally involved with Hester?

'So?' she prompted.

'If I tell you that I shall never say or do anything to hurt Hester, will that satisfy you? My feelings for her are very deep.'

Lydia knew that he had dealt subtly with the situation while not giving anything away, and although she had taken him into her confidence about Clive, he had studiously avoided mentioning Vivien, or their meal together, to say nothing of the arrangement with Hester. Confidences had never been obligatory and only sporadically indulged, but somehow this time she felt strangely shut out.

Lance got up from his desk and came around to where she was standing by the door. The faint suggestion of warmth came in a wave from his body and, with it, the unmistakable smell of ether, which clung after a hospital visit to attend the operation on a patient of his. In those seconds Lydia was totally conscious of his nearness.

'Mind if I pop in for a drink later on?' he asked. 'I want to discuss Mrs Berkley's thyrotoxicosis, for one thing; and for another, it's a luxury to relax and be able to talk to someone with whom one isn't expected to go to bed!' A smile hovered on his lips.

Subconsciously, Lydia thought of Vivien. Had she expected that demonstration?

'On the contrary. . . make it about six-thirty.' Lydia avoided meeting his gaze and hurried to her consulting room.

Odile Craig came in looking drawn, scared, hesitant, and not at all the defiant teenager Lydia had anticipated. On the few occasions Lydia had previously seen her for minor complaints, she had been boldly aggressive, knowing all the answers. Her hair was mid-brown and fashionably untidy, but shining.

She hadn't any make-up on, her skin was pale and her large normally lustrous eyes were dull and hunted.

'Now,' said Lydia encouragingly, as they both sat down, 'you want to see me.' Her gaze was kind and friendly.

'You've talked to Mum. . .'

'Yes.'

There was a sudden silence which Odile broke by crying out, 'She doesn't *know*... You see, I'm pregnant.' A little wail escaped her. 'I'm terrified! What can I do with a baby? I don't even *like* them!'

Lydia didn't make the obvious remark that it was a little late to take that into account. All she could think of was the desperation and desolation of Alma Craig and her husband, two people who had worked hard to build up a now thriving newsagents and general store.

'Pregnant,' Odile repeated, the word coming with a shudder. 'It's six weeks since my last period and it's been hell. . . there hasn't been a *minute*. . . the awful waiting and hoping.'

'Six weeks is by no means certain,' Lydia suggested professionally.

'I've told myself that. I brought the subject of contraception up with Mum deliberately, so that I'd be able to come to you; and she didn't rave, or give me a lot of that moral stuff.'

'You *do* realise,' said Lydia, her gaze unnerving, 'how worried she is about you? You're under age, Odile. Did you imagine you could deceive everyone by talking about going on the pill, and somehow, miraculously, arrange to have an abortion?'

Colour flamed into the pale cheeks. That was precisely what had been in that girl's mind.

'But what am I going to *do?* Oh, Dr Richmond, help me—please help me! I've been such a fool. I thought it was clever to do what others in the group were doing, going along with their switched-on trendy ideas.' Odile lowered her head as she muttered, 'I didn't even *like* it, but I daren't say so. He was rough. . . it was just sex—' She spoke with distaste. Then she rushed on, 'There are a lot of girls like me who haven't the courage to—to cut it all out and be themselves. We must be one of a crowd. I thought I could be like that. . . when all the time I was just weak and stupid. Now some of them are on drugs. If the teachers and parents knew—'

Lydia said with a sharp fear, 'You're not on drugs?'

There was no doubting the truth of the cry, 'No; I'm scared—and now, with *this*. . . I used to be so happy; my parents are super and I've treated them—well, just rotten. And, Dr Richmond, I'm not just being square because I'm frightened. . . It all stinks! I wanted to go to university, and I've ruined everything. For what? And all the time the boys are conning you. I feel I never want to be touched again. When it comes to it—well, it's like agreeing to rape!' She gave a little sob.

'Let me examine you first,' Lydia said quietly, 'so we know a little where we are.' Lydia did not ring for Nurse Webster, as she often did on such occasions, feeling she would sustain Odile's confidence if they were alone.

Despite her experience, Odile felt nervous and embarrassed as she climbed on to the examining couch, pulling the sheet high up to her neck and looking at Lydia with a rather woebegone appealing expression. The mature, sophisticated and defiant 'woman' had gone, and in its place was a frightened, desperate fifteen-year-old whose life appeared to be in ruins.

With the penetration for the pelvic examination, Lydia said suddenly, 'You're bleeding; your period has started.' She added, 'The fact that you're late isn't uncommon in cases like this. The upheaval, shock—'

But Odile was crying silently, tears running unchecked down her cheeks, an expression of thankfulness transforming her face as she gasped, the truth sinking in, 'To be. . .' a sob caught at her throat, 'out of *hell*—'

Lydia rang for Nurse Webster and said gently, touching Odile's shoulder, 'Nurse will look after you and give you all you need, and when you're dressed we'll talk.'

'Now,' Lydia began as Odile faced her some short while later, 'you've had a lucky escape. But where are you going from here?'

'Never back to that kind of life. . .oh, I know you can't help thinking that in a little while I'll forget all this, be back here, or that I'm going to ask you for a contraceptive; but,' she added fiercely, 'I'm not. I'm under age and I'm going to live that way. At the moment sex disgusts me. . .to think of all I've been through. . .for what? Not love, that's for certain. I want to look my parents in the face again and not fight them because of my own cheapness and guilt.' A maturity seeped through the former wildness. 'Oh, I'm not the cringing penitent, Dr Richmond; I'm just disgusted because I could be such a *fool!*' Her voice rang with conviction and then dropped to an apprehensive whisper. 'I don't want them to know about all this. . .you won't tell Mum?'

'You're my patient, Odile; nothing goes beyond these four walls. . . *Now* you say you'll finish with this kind of existence and remember that you're under age, but if they're just words—'

'They're not! Oh, they're *not*. I'll never sleep around again.' Odile looked shamefaced. 'It wasn't quite that, but I was getting to feel dirty. I don't want any contraceptives.' She hurried on, 'When I'm older and if there's someone special. . .' She gave a little shudder of distaste. 'At the moment I can't imagine ever *wanting* anyone. I'd be scared anyway after this.'

Fear, Lydia thought, was often the safest pill, and she said firmly, 'I want you to keep in touch with me. I'm here to help you; talk through anything—*anything*. Don't let this influence you. And remember that your mother is the best friend you have. She's proved it, by coming to me herself and agreeing for you to do so.'

'Oh, I know; I know. I've been foul to her—a proper bitch,' Odile added in disgust. 'Why I let myself get in with. . . weak. I wanted to prove I was as smart—' She looked at Lydia with a half-apologetic gaze. 'You must think I'm just a stupid kid who needed teaching a lesson—God, I've had the lesson all right! What shall I tell Mum?'

'That we've discussed contraception and are agreed that it isn't necessary because you're not ready to experiment, and want to get on with your work.' Lydia fixed her with a warning look. 'Always assuming that *is* what you really intend.'

'Oh, it is! I swear it! These last two weeks—everything. . . drinking, smoking, lying; a friend, younger than me, had an abortion.' A little shudder went over the girl's youthful body and panic flashed in her eyes. 'What I've escaped—'

Lydia felt sad. It was like looking at flawed Dresden, but she accepted that this shock might be more salutary than admonition.

Odile's mood changed. 'Life's not an easy game, anyway,' she said. 'Grown-ups make a big enough mess of it, too. . . I suppose that's a good reason for having a few years without responsibility when you're in your teens. Half of us have been scared stiff and lost all our self-respect. You've been very patient, listening to me and—and everything. The nurse was super, too. Oh, Dr Richmond, I *am* grateful—'

'Then set your sights on university; make up for lost time—you've got your life ahead, Odile. Don't wreck it.'

Odile's eyes were suspiciously bright.

'Steer by your parents' example; you won't go far wrong and you'll *enjoy* it all, and make up to them for the anxiety you've caused. I'm not preaching, believe me—'

'I know; doctors see everything—'

'See everything,' Lydia sighed. 'That's true enough.' She thought of herself and Lance. Their failure suddenly became a hurt.

When Lydia left Carisbrooke House soon after Odile had gone, she bumped into Vivien as she reached the front door.

'Is Lance still here?' asked Vivien.

'No.' Lydia stepped out on to the porch. She could have explained that Lance had gone to St Joseph's to see a patient, but she didn't want to begin a conversation and sought protection in the monosyllable. 'See you,' she added, and moved hurriedly away.

The sun struck her as she walked to the mews, but the flat was cool, aided by the awnings which protected it from the heat and gave it a continental air, bright and festive. The windowboxes of the other houses and flats created a garden-like effect and removed any drab city atmosphere. It occurred to her, as she showered and changed into a loose kaftan-type dress of light cherry and white silk, that she had entertained Clive, Steven and, on several occasions, Lance, her reactions to each one entirely different and stimulating varied emotions. Lance seemed the most intriguing, for he was returning to what had once been his own home. It was difficult to believe that she had fallen in love with him, fallen out of love, and that they had stabilised a friendship which was both satisfying and sincere.

She didn't want to dwell on the physical attraction that had recently manifested itself, regarding it as a transitory phase having no significance.

His car drew up on the cobbled stones, for he had driven to and from the hospital near Gower Street, where he had seen a fourteen-year-old boy, Tommy West, on whom he had operated for appendicitis the previous day.

Lydia admitted him with easy familiarity and he followed her into the sitting room, and walked naturally to the drinks tray.

'Hot—thirsty!' he exclaimed.

'There's some white wine in the fridge.'

'Oh, splendid!'

Lydia fetched it and they both drank gratefully, smiling and relaxing in their respective chairs.

'Tommy all right?' she asked.

'Fine.' He looked at the windows and back to her. 'I'd forgotten how quiet it is here.'

She was aware of the implication and hastened, 'Well, we're off the beaten track inasmuch as Banks Road diverts the bulk of the traffic.'

Neither reacted to her use of the word, 'we'.

Lance sighed contentedly and stretched himself, his long limbs emphasising his tall figure and fine body. She tried not to be aware of his movements, or his attractive features above the cream shirt and linen jacket.

His gaze met hers, frankly admiring.

'I like the Eastern effect of your dress. Looks very cool, and suits you.'

'Thank you.'

'Mrs Berkley,' he exclaimed in typical doctor fashion, patients often taking precedence even in the most intimate conversations.

'The thyroid case?' Lydia clicked into his mood.

'I hope Bob Maxton hasn't taken just a little too much of the gland away when he operated.'

'Oh!' Lydia understood. Three-quarters of the gland could be removed and the quarter left usually produced enough thyroxine to stabilise the situation. 'And Mrs Berkley is very anti drugs of any kind.'

'A charming woman, but a difficult patient,' said Lance, sipping his wine. 'But we shall see. As she gets older she'll need some extra thyroid-hormone supplements, anyway. She still gets very excitable and drops off to sleep at the wrong time.'

'Not always easy to separate the complaint from the temperamental idiosyncrasies: the two can simulate each other,' Lydia suggested.

'How true that is. . . I regret not specialising,' he added. 'Being a general surgeon makes me a dogsbody.'

'But you are excellent at it,' she insisted.

'I ought to have followed in Edward's footsteps.'

'Specialising in gynaecology?'

'Not necessarily; just specialising in *something*.'

'I didn't think you wanted Harley Street any more than your father wants it. . . he's a very special person in every field—particularly as a human being. As

I've said so many times, I'm very lucky to have him and Marion as my friends still.'

'You're like their daughter. The "ex" doesn't come into it. Whatever happened between us would never change that, and I don't think we're likely to fall out now,' he finished in a firm, rather enticing tone.

Lydia took the opportunity of bringing up a subject that had concerned her since the discussion with Clive, as she asked shatteringly, 'How would you feel if, in the event of my marrying Clive, I also joined him in Edward's practice—became the third member, junior member, of the team?'

Lance's hand jerked some of the wine from his glass, spilling it on the carpet as he gave a little gasp of astonishment.

'That's a leading question if you like!' He put his glass down on the side table. 'You know what I think about Clive in relation to you, but when it comes to *working*. . . I've tried to reconcile myself to your leaving Carisbrooke, but to transfer to Heath Edge— become part of *that* set-up—' He got to his feet restlessly, thrusting his hands in his pockets in a gesture of frustration, his features hardening.

Lydia rushed in, 'Don't misunderstand, Lance. . . nothing has ever been said by your father.'

'Meaning the idea was Clive's?' The question was sharp.

'Yes; but we didn't go *into* it. I just got the impression that the possibility had been discussed.'

'That's understandable and fair enough. . . and how do you feel about the prospect?'

'Interested,' she admitted. 'It would be an honour to work for Edward and, obviously, if I were married to Clive the situation would be ideal—' She paused and they looked at each other intently as Lance sat down again. 'You haven't expressed any real opinion—'

'Since I can only be the loser,' he commented, 'what do you expect me to say? It makes the evil day when we split up our working relationship, seem perilously close. But that doesn't mean I'm lost to the advantages from your point of view—or theirs. They certainly need more help.' He sighed deeply. 'God knows, so shall I when you go.'

They looked at each other and there was an inevitability in their expression, and a mounting tension. Both in that moment felt allergic to the possibility of change.

'I want you to find the right person *before* I go,' she insisted. 'I shan't be married tomorrow, in any case.'

'Neither will you wait a year,' he said, studying her as he spoke. 'Funny to be sitting here talking about your possible second husband. Intriguing situation, too, if you eventually work for your ex-father-in-law!'

'No less intriguing than my working for you,' she reminded him, his penetrating gaze awakening emotion that quickened her heart beat. It was disconcerting to be so physically aware of him, while having no illusions about their relationship.

'I suppose that's true.' He continued to study her with disturbing intensity. 'I'll look for someone for the practice—'

She interrupted him, 'But I thought you'd been looking, *were* looking—' It was an admonition.

Lance made a little apologetic gesture, 'Half-heartedly and in a very critical mood, I must admit! But I promise you one thing: when I see an engagement ring on your finger, I'll soon get fixed up.' He made it sound very simple.

Lydia stared him out.

'And when *you* get engaged?' She spoke in the tone of one who didn't intend to be put off.

There was a sudden heavy silence, his expression darkened as he said a trifle sharply, 'When I marry again, it won't affect my professional life, I assure you.'

'No more doctors in the family,' she said lightly, refusing to be put off by his attitude.

'Suppose we wait and see,' he suggested with finality, and immediately changed the subject.

Lydia had the unsatisfactory feeling that he had evaded giving her a direct answer to her original question, but had left her with the impression that the idea of her working with Clive concerned him far more than the possibility of her marrying him. All of which was symptomatic of their bizarre relationship.

When he had finished his second glass of wine, Lydia said, 'I'm having a cold supper. . . if you would like to join me—'

He said quickly, 'I told Mrs Carson I'd be in, thanks all the same. Also, I shall run over to see Hester afterwards.'

Lydia asked herself, had she really lived with this man? Been his wife, slept with him, accepted compromise at so many levels and yet, now, was so physically conscious of him that were he to attempt to make love to her, she doubted if she would have any power of resistance. The reflection brought colour to her cheeks and made her hands tremble. There was no question of love coming into it, and that shocked her, revealing a side of her nature she would have previously considered foreign.

She accepted his reply as an indication that he was about to leave, and got to her feet with an easy understanding. He stood beside her, arms almost touching, a menacing aggression suddenly manifesting itself as he bent swiftly, his lips parting hers in a hard passionate kiss which ended abruptly, while he stood back, aware of her response.

Then, like an actor skilfully throwing a line away, he said, 'I told you that these warm summer evenings were sensuous and tempting.'

CHAPTER FIVE

LYDIA was unnerved by the fact that she had responded to Lance's kiss and that he was aware of it.

'I remember,' she said lightly, avoiding his gaze and realising immediately that he was relieved because no explanation was expected.

The doorbell rang, making her jump, but she was grateful for the interruption and went swiftly to answer it.

'Steven!' Her voice rose in surprise.

Lance strolled from the sitting room to the lobby.

'Hello,' he said pleasantly, wondering if Steven was a frequent visitor. 'I was just going.' He looked at Lydia, at ease as he added, making for the front door and with one hand on the latch, 'Thanks for the drink. . . 'Bye, Steven.'

Back in the sitting room, Steven looked a little uncomfortable.

'Have I barged in?' he asked.

'Good heavens, no! Lance was about to leave.' She tried to collect her thoughts, behave naturally, but the shattering experience of Lance's kiss left her bewildered and mystified. She knew, with embarrassment, that had it lasted even a second longer, her arms would have been around his neck.

Steven shot her an observant glance. He would never understand her relationship with Lance, and suspicion lurked behind his acceptance. He could not dismiss the possibility of it being a question of having an ex-wife as a mistress, the idea intrigued him, although, he argued, Lydia was too transparent and honest to be able to sustain such a deception, even if it were feasible.

'I wondered if you felt like going to La Pavona?' Lydia teased, 'Not often you're at a loose end!'

'Touché!' He looked faintly apologetic. The accusation had a grain of truth in it. Vivien had refused him because she had an important telephone call to make.

Lydia was frank. 'Stay and have a drink, and then I want a quiet evening on my own. I'm not in the mood for a restaurant, even one as good as La Pavona.'

'Fair enough,' he agreed.

Meanwhile Vivien was ringing Lance, who had called in at his flat to see if there were any messages, and took the call somewhat apprehensively. Would he like to walk around for a coffee and brandy a little later on?

'I'm just going to see Hester,' he explained. 'How about a show tomorrow evening, if you're free?'

She made a pretence of looking through her diary and then accepted. Things couldn't be progressing more smoothly between herself and Lance, she thought with a thrill of satisfaction, and she was wise enough not to prolong the conversation. They'd finalise the arrangements tomorrow.

It was a fortnight later when Lance said to Lydia, 'We'll all be getting together at Heath Edge this Sunday, I understand. You and Clive; and Hester's staying the weekend. Vivien and I are taking her to Aldbury in the afternoon.'

'Buckinghamshire,' said Lydia, a strange sensation in the pit of her stomach. 'Actually Hester told

me you were going.' There was something in the way
he uttered Vivien's name that alerted Lydia. She had
no illusions about Vivien's interest in Lance, but on
reflection, she realised that Vivien's name had crept
insidiously into conversations during the past weeks
and had a new significance.

There was an uneasy silence, which Lance broke
by saying a little shortly, 'Nothing secret about it. The
idea came up when I took Vivien to the theatre. . .
why don't you join us?'

Lydia's laugh was a little high-pitched. 'Aren't two
women enough?'

He frowned.

'You're in a strange mood,' he said critically.

Lydia couldn't deny it. She had the uneasy feeling
that Vivien's interest in Hester was solely to impress
Lance, and the situation made her suspicious. Added
to which was the fugitive fear lest Vivien might be
instrumental in causing dissension. One false move
on her, Lydia's, part could be catastrophic. Lance's
friendships, as she had so often stressed, had nothing
to do with her, and she found herself wishing that his
feelings for Hester were of a more romantic nature.

She said swiftly and apologetically, 'I'm sorry; it
was an unfounded remark.'

'I should hate our friendship to be endangered,
Lydia. Don't hold my impulsive behaviour that evening against me,' he added significantly, the incident
not having been mentioned previously. 'I don't go
around indiscriminately kissing alluring ladies, I
assure you.'

Both knew they were on dangerous ground, since
his behaviour had met with her response. The atmosphere was tense as she commented, 'And I don't go
around indiscriminately kissing attractive men,

either. . . Summer evenings are responsible for a great many emotional follies.'

'Ah!' His sigh was relieved.

They were standing in the centre of Lance's room, about to snatch a short break for lunch, when the intercom went and Nurse Webster said hurriedly, 'Mr Martin. Urgent.'

Lance took the call immediately. Charles Martin said his wife was having contractions.

'I'll come at once.' The receiver went down briskly, and Lance flicked the intercom and spoke to Nurse Webster. 'Ring Mr Jones and tell him I've been called urgently to Mrs Martin; then get on to St Joseph's and advise them I'll be sending her in. Speak to Sister Bennet, Private Wing.'

Elsa Martin had been determined to have a second child, since her first was stillborn, and although she had heart failure associated with mitral valve disease—a narrowing of the mitral valve of the heart—refused to consider a termination. Mark Jones, famous consultant gynaecologist, had been engaged for the delivery in hospital and Lance had taken care of her, under his supervision, throughout the pregnancy. She'd had every possible test, including an echocardiagram (ultrasound), complete bed rest, digoxin with care; her fluids reduced and diuretics to enable her to pass more water.

Lance had picked up his medical bag, his manner urgent as he said to Lydia, 'We were sending her in this weekend, anyway; she's due in three weeks. Pray God there aren't any complications . . . Come with me. You've been on the case and there's only Sally Miles, apart from the staff, there.'

Lydia understood. Sally had her diploma of nursing and had been a companion-cum-factotumduring these months, but could not be expected to take responsibility in an emergency, although she would be of great assistance.

Lydia nodded her agreement, and having arranged with Mrs Trent for the manipulation of their appointments, hurried with him out into the street and so to his car. The muscles of his face were set, his expression grave. He was thinking that if there was any question of a protracted labour, Mark Jones would induce her. He felt, however, that he was dealing with dynamite.

They reached the Martin house—a white colonnaded building overlooking Regent's Park—in a matter of minutes, having broken the speed limit. Charles Martin greeted them immediately they were admitted. He was standing at the bottom of a wide sweeping staircase, its panelled and beaded walls hung with valuable paintings. He was a charming tycoon of thirty-five, tall, slim, and now white-faced, who loved his wife deeply.

'Thank God you're here!' he cried. 'Since I telephoned, Sally says the waters have broken.'

Lance went up the stairs two at a time.

Elsa Martin was lying in a large bed—in an equally large, white-carpeted room—with a padded peach satin headboard and matching frilled duvet. Her eyes wide, dark and frightened. She was twenty-six, and beautiful in a frail porcelain fashion.

She spoke with a certain effort, faintly breathless. 'The baby. . . I mustn't lose the baby.' Her hands went out almost in supplication as she looked at Lance and Lydia. 'Help me; please help me!'

Lance had hurried into the adjoining bathroom to wash his hands, Lydia's fingers went on the patient's pulse. Charles Martin held his wife's right hand, having no intention of leaving.

Sally Miles, quiet, efficient, met Lydia's gaze as she busied herself with all the equipment that had been acquired for any emergency. Silence held the breath of fear.

The moment Lance began his examination, he realised that the first stage of labour, where the neck of the uterus dilated to about four inches, had passed. He looked up at Sally in surprise and she nodded as she said, 'You'll never know how thankful I am you're here. It's going to be quick.'

They were in a swift second stage, where the baby was pushed from the pelvis down through the vagina. There was no question of having time to get the patient to hospital: the birth was already taking place—Lydia supportive, with Charles Martin at his wife's side. Finally Lance eased the child into the world, sparing the need for an episiotomy, a cut in the floor of the pelvis. Mercifully labour had been speedy and the effect on the heart minimal by normal standards.

'You've got a son,' Lance told him joyously, 'and he's fine!'

Tears were running gently, happily and gratefully, down the mother's face, her exhaustion of no account as the baby was placed in her arms, and she and the father peered down at it as though looking upon a miracle.

'Oh, thank you; just thank you!' It was a breathless tribute as Elsa Martin looked at Lance and Lydia, sparing a glance for Sally. 'I won't have to go to hospital now, will I?'

'No,' Lance said gently. 'Sally's going to make you comfortable and I shall come back to see you in a very short while.' The heart had been relieved of the burden of pregnancy and Elsa would begin to adjust to a fairly normal life under supervision and digoxin;

meanwhile she had to recover from the immediate strain.

Downstairs, Lance said with some urgency, 'I have a trained nurse ready to take over, obviously with your permission, Mr Martin. This swift labour is something I didn't foresee, but for which I made tentative provision. Nurse Walters knows of the circumstances, and I've only to ring her. She's just retired, but is taking a few cases because she loves the work so much. You must remember that the baby is three weeks premature and underweight, in any case, although he doesn't need to be in an incubator he needs special care.'

Charles Martin flung out his hands. 'Anyone—anything; you have only to tell me what you want. Of course Sally couldn't manage alone.'

'But she will be invaluable in helping Nurse Walters. If I could telephone her, she could come in today.' Lance added, 'Mr Jones will be along the moment he can. He's already been contacted. I am sure that without a trained nurse, he would insist on hospital care for your wife.' Lance congratulated himself that he had allowed for all emergencies.

'How is she—*really*, Dr Richmond?' It was an anxious, appealing enquiry.

'She's come through it remarkably well,' Lance assured him. 'She's escaped pulmonary congestion and oedema, and with proper convalescence life will have a new meaning. I'm going to have a look at her now, and satisfy myself before we have that drink.'

At that moment Lance glanced at Lydia, who had remained sympathetically silent during the conversation. This was a situation they had not experienced together in their married life, and neither knew if regret lay behind their steady gaze.

When they left the house a little later it was with the knowledge that their patient was stable and asleep, the baby, Toby by name, was satisfactory and Nurse Walters delighted to be on her way.

It had been a lunch hour and more well spent.

There was a quiet sympathy and understanding between Clive and Hester as they sat swaying gently on the cushioned hammock in the garden at Heath Edge. They did not need continual conversation and their silences were harmonious—a communication they both valued.

'Are there any clouds?' asked Hester. 'Somehow I don't think so, the air is too soft and warm and the sunlight doesn't vary. . . a perfect summer day?'

'A perfect summer day,' Clive repeated. 'We've had a fortnight, and even if we pay for it—'

'The memory will be there. . . it's a pity we forget the good things. . . it's lovely here with Edward and Marion. I often think it's the safest place in the world. They make you feel you *belong*.' She gave a gentle but happy sigh. 'This is more home to me than the flat, you know. . . Lance has just come back from his emergency patient.'

'I can't see him,' Clive said, naturally.

'Oh, it's just that I know the sound of his car. He stops differently from the others. You all drive and stop differently.' Hester gave a little laugh. 'You really *do* miss a lot!' She knew he was waiting for Lydia, she could almost feel him watching the house and door to the patio which was nearby, just as she was longing to hear Lance's voice, hear his 'Hello, Hester', as though her being there was important. 'That's Lydia; her door makes a special bang. Steven and Vivien are going to be last.' She didn't like the fact that she wished Vivien were not coming. There was a rather frightened feeling when she was with her, as though her security and confidence had gone. Vivien was, in fact, the one person who made her *feel* blind. But she dismissed the unpleasant thoughts and, turning her face to Clive, said, 'You go and see Lydia.'

Clive got to his feet and touched Hester's shoulder. They did not need to be politely formal.

'I will,' he said brightly. 'And here comes Lance,' he added as he moved away.

Hester greeted Lance with, 'Anyone would know you'd come from hospital!' She held out her left hand, which he grasped with his.

'What an advertisement!' he laughed, and looked around him.

Hester said almost instinctively, 'Vivien hasn't arrived yet.'

But at that moment, Lance saw her car in the near distance of the drive. She was within shouting distance and waved as she began the short walk to the hammock. On this occasion she wore black and white—a patterned material, with a V-shaped neckline, having interchanging colours.

'Hello,' she said, stooping to brush Hester's cheek and then met Lance's gaze with a little intimate smile. 'And hello, Dr Richmond. It's a perfect day and this is a perfect setting.'

'I should always recognise you,' said Hester, a shade of laughter in her voice.

'How?' It was a half-fearful question.

'Your scent—just a faint trace.'

'Body lotion,' Vivien said uncompromisingly. 'I shall have to vary it,' She gave a rather hard laugh. 'Like having a detective around, isn't it Lance?'

'Everyone can smell fragrance,' Hester murmured.

Vivien made no comment but held Lance's gaze, and they exchanged an understanding look. Vivien was irritated by Hester's presence when she could otherwise have had a few minutes alone with Lance.

'Edward is just bringing out the drinks on the patio,' Hester remarked, a few minutes later.

Vivien cried, 'Good heavens, how can you possibly tell?' It was a spontaneous reaction this time, which Hester accepted.

'The sound of his footsteps; he puts one foot down a little heavier than the other and he's moving slowly—people don't rush when they're carrying trays and glasses, and perhaps bottles, too. And I know the time.'

Vivien made a gesture of near-disbelief.

'You're quite incredible!' she exclaimed, and would like to have added, 'and uncanny'. She found Hester's perception unnerving.

'Let's make a move,' said Lance.

Hester picked up her long cane, a hollow tube of light aluminium alloy which had a rubber grip and a curved handle—the tip was made of nylon and replaceable—and made her way with the others, negotiating the three steps from the lawns to the patio expertly.

Lydia sat down beside Clive in a comfortable wicker chair and watched the three of them with interest. Lance looked both relaxed and happy, and Vivien exuded self-satisfied charm. Any man, Lydia reflected, would be attracted to her, and she always managed to look just right no matter what the occasion. Lance had removed his jacket and his shirt sleeves were rolled up, giving him a casual appearance that was attractive.

'I've made some Pimms,' Edward said brightly, indicating a large frosted jug garnished with borage, cucumber and all the necessities.

Marion appeared from the kitchen where she had been busy cooking. Hester had sat and talked to her, deploring the fact that without her own domestic working gadgets in Braille, she was not a great deal of help, although skilful at preparing items for decoration. An old-fashioned Sunday lunch was being laid on, sirloin and all the trimmings. As Hester said, 'Bunty and I can never really have a joint because we don't want a large one, and it just isn't the same with a measly little piece. And no one makes a Yorkshire pudding like yours that rises to the top of the oven!'

And while the choice was not ideal for a hot day, everyone appreciated it nevertheless.

Marion sat down with the happy sigh of a woman who has got a meal under control and could relax with impunity.

'Pimms, darling,' she said to Edward as he put her glass down on the table in front of her, 'is just what the doctor ordered. Long and cool!'

'Must look after the cook.' he said with a grin. 'I don't care if it's a hot day and rabbit food is the thing, I'm looking forward to a proper *meal*. I missed breakfast with Mrs Best deciding to go into labour before I could tackle my bacon and eggs—'

Vivien said, 'You, a doctor, eating all the wrong things!'

'Sunday is my "treats" day,' he said with a whimsical humour. 'Besides, Hester and I need nourishment and like the same things!' He looked at Vivien with a direct gaze. 'You disapprove?'

'How could I disapprove of anything when your wife is such an expert cook!'

'Such diplomacy!' chuckled Edward, realising suddenly that Vivien had sampled quite a bit of Marion's cooking recently and, a little to his dismay, Lydia and Clive less.

'Your health is a good testimonial,' Vivien exclaimed.

Edward looked tanned and attractive as he stood there, and just then Lydia thought how alike he and Lance were. Clive cut into her reflective gaze and she looked away quickly.

Hester held her glass in her hand and kept it there without realising that, apart from when she was drinking, her face was turned to Lance. . . He sat beside her and she longed to stretch out her hand and touch his, her love for him both ecstasy and pain. Half of her wanted to go out that afternoon; the other half shrank from being with Vivien, who had the effect of silencing her and making her feel inadequate mentally, so that where normally she would talk brightly and humorously, she now sat quietly sub-dued.

'Steven's late,' Vivien said suddenly.

His car reached the drive at that moment and he strode from it across the lawn to the patio, which flanked the side of the house.

'Sorry I'm late,' he apologised to Marion. 'I over-slept.' He greeted everyone, kissing Hester's hand, and cut through an awkward silence.

Clive had hoped Steven wouldn't arrive. Although he had no illusions about Lydia's feelings for him, nevertheless he recognised that a man of his type was always a threat. He would be there at the appropri-ate moment to soothe, or inflame. For him the grass would always be greener over there, and his unden-iable easy charm a menace. On the other hand, Clive

acknowledged that his behaviour to Hester was irre-
proachable. He teased and sometimes flattered her,
but she could never misunderstand him.

It was a very successful meal, and Steven contrib-
uted a great deal to the conversation. Lance's
reactions to him had a good deal in common with
Clive's, although at a slightly different level. And as
he sat there, Lance found himself pondering on the
possibility of Lydia joining the Hampstead practice
and marrying Clive. It had not been discussed further, and since Lydia had told him in confidence, he
was not at liberty to broach the subject either to his
father, or to Clive, as he would like to have done.

'Busy?' he asked deliberately in a moment of
silence, looking from his father to Clive.

'That's the understatement of the year,' Edward
retorted, and flashed Clive a meaningful look.

'One,' said Clive firmly, 'that must soon be
resolved.' His gaze rested on Lydia's face and his eyes
met hers with a challenging expression which, inter-
preted, might have said, 'I want your answer; this
situation can't drag on.'

Marion was troubled by the position in the practice. Both Edward and Clive worked far too hard, but
she appreciated their reluctance to take on a partner
precipitately, since harmony and excellence couldn't
be guaranteed. She wished Lance had felt like joining
them, but knew that had always been a pipe dream.
The three men were the best of friends, but they had
clashing temperaments when in sustained proximity.

'I would like to have been a doctor,' said Hester,
'but I *could* have done your job, Vivien. There are a
lot of blind physiotherapists, all sorts of jobs for people like me. Gardening, piano-tuning. . . I don't
know why I thought of that—' She gave a little laugh.
'Mr Murrow who tunes my piano is blind; we have

some wonderful talks when he comes, and we can discuss all the gadgets on the market adapted in Braille, and—' She stopped. She could *feel* Viviens's gaze upon her and it made her self-conscious. 'But that isn't very interesting,' she hastened. . . 'Oh, Marion, that was a lovely lunch,' she added irrelevantly and with enthusiasm.

Clive said gently, 'You would have made a splendid doctor—perhaps a little too sympathetic and concerned.'

'Can one be that?' asked Hester, her head slightly to one side as she turned in his direction. 'Lance is both—and Lydia.'

'A satisfied patient,' Vivien interposed, smiling at Lance with a little possessive air. She turned to Lydia, glancing, also, at Clive. 'And what are you doing this afternoon?'

'Lazing,' Lydia replied.

'And reading the newspaper,' added Clive. He turned to Lance, 'I expect you'll have a cup of tea, out somewhere?'

'Probably at the Copper Kettle.' He looked at Steven. 'Feel like joining us?'

Vivien seemed alerted, but she didn't speak.

'Thanks, I'd enjoy it. Good heavens, I haven't been out into the country for God knows how long!'

'I stick to the country lanes,' Lance warned him. 'It's not my idea of fun to be tearing along the motorways in order to get to one's destination unless, of course, it's necessary.'

They set off about three. Clive and Lydia sauntered to the drive with them and stood while Lance told Hester which way the car was facing, and that she would be sitting in the front. He then put her hand on the door handle and she got into the seat unaided.

The vital thing was to do the little things that gave the blind independence and caused the least fuss. Lance was, Lydia thought as she watched, an excellent, unobtrusive guide. Vivien could not appreciate why Hester liked being in a car, indifferent to the fact that the movement, open windows, the breeze on her face in its varying strength, and the power of the sun, told her a great deal about the country through which they were passing. And she was hyper-sensitive when it came to the smell of the different trees, of the nearness of forest or woods.

Aldbury was less than thirty miles away on the Buckinghamshire border, in a beautiful valley near Ashridge Park. A village green and pond, plus a giant elm tree, gave it an atmosphere of antiquity which the parish church of St John the Baptist fostered, since it mostly dated back to the fifteenth century. Ancient stocks and a whipping-post completed a picture that whispered of the past. Having walked around the village, Hester tracing various objects with her fingers, rather as a magnificent pianist might caress the keys, they took the road to Ashridge Park, through the woods which led to Aldbury Common, a large open space of trees and bracken.

'Bracken!' sighed Hester. 'It always smells so good. We're outside Ashridge Park—I always know, because we came up that very steep hill just now.'

'Thank heaven the National Trust bought all this,' Lance remarked, 'or we shouldn't be enjoying it now.'

'There are two thousand, four hundred and fifty-eight acres, including Ivinghoe Beacon and Berkhampstead Common in the Ashridge Estate,' Hester said easily. 'Bunty read to me about it. I wish one had a wider choice of travel books in Braille. And Moon takes up so much more room—'

'What is Moon?' asked Vivien. 'Like Braille?'

'Yes—embossed writing, based on a series of raised geometric shapes, larger, easier to learn and feel.' Hester gave a little regretful sigh. 'Unfortunately it's bulkier than Braille and needs a special printing press to produce it, so you can't write it at home!'

The wind gusted slightly and ruffled her hair; the smell of ripening crops, the lullaby of the breeze skimming over hedgerow and blossom, filled her with delight as she listened, and cried, 'Oh, Lance, it's wonderful to be out like this.'

'But you go out in the car with Bunty,' Vivien exclaimed, and added, fearful of striking the wrong note, 'but it's different on a day like this—special.' She could see Lance's face in the driving mirror and his expression denoted his obvious pleasure that she was drawing Hester out. From her own point of view it was vital for the afternoon to be a success.

Hester said without hesitation, 'Yes, it's special on a day like this.' She was thinking of being with Lance, not just for a little while, but secure in the knowledge that not only was he beside her now, but that the whole evening lay ahead.

They stopped later at the Copper Kettle, near Little Gaddesden, its old-fashioned atmosphere preserved even to the waitresses' dresses, with frills, tight bodices and full skirts. Lance guided Hester in through the narrow doorway and passage, by putting his guiding arm behind her back, so that she could follow and hold on to him while he made his steps shorter, and when they reached the tea room itself, steered her towards the door on the handle side. Once they had selected their table he put Hester's hand on the back of her chair, enabling her to lower herself down, rather than be bundled on to it like a parcel. Her cane was not necessary since she had his assistance.

'A lovely smell,' she said. 'They have log fires here in the winter.'

'Oh, you know it?' queried Vivien and shot Lance a questioning look.

'This is my first visit, but the smell of wood and smoke—I'm sure there are logs stacked in a chimney corner. There's an atmosphere of beams, low ceilings. . . I can tell by the air. And that passageway we came through told me it was very old.'

'Late seventeenth century,' Lance told her. 'I've been meaning to bring you here.' He added self-critically, 'This summer is flying. I hardly know what I've been doing during these past weeks!'

Steven sat there intrigued by the expression on Vivien's face. She was very much the hostess whose proprietorial attitude towards Lance was noticeable.

Hester discreetly spread her fingers over the crockery—fingertip assessment—and when the tea was brought she seemed to measure distance with an amazing accuracy while Vivien watched, fascinated. The only request she made was that her cup should be half-filled. Her movements had the delicacy of a magician's hands and were used as dexterously. Later, back in the car, she gave a little appreciative sigh.

'That was lovely,' she said, her face turned to Lance. 'I feel I've been back in history. . . the waitresses were wearing full skirts; I could hear the swish as they moved about.'

Lance described them, reflecting how thoughtless the sighted were, taking everything for granted; but it was not easy to strike just the right balance and avoid emphasising the blindness by too much detailed description. And with Hester it was so easy to believe that she could see.

Steven said, 'If anyone had told me I should enjoy an outing like this, I should have thought they were crazy.' He looked around him at the cottage gardens as he got back into the car.

Hester detailed the flowers—roses, old-fashioned pinks, stocks—their fragrance her special language, her world of imagination where touch had given the blossoms form and shape, making them real.

'It's been a happy afternoon,' said Vivien, a note in her voice with which one would address a child.

'I wonder if we could make up a party and go to see *Forty-Second Street,*' Hester said a little later. 'It's ages since I went to the theatre, and if you haven't seen it. . . Clive and Lydia love the theatre, too.' In that moment she wanted to have an objective, something to which to look forward that would involve Lance.

'Splendid,' he said with enthusiasm. 'We'll do something about it—have supper afterwards and make a celebration of it.'

Vivien added her approval, wondering why Hester would find pleasure in watching something she couldn't see, forgetting that the atmosphere, the contact with other people. the voices from the stage— even the smell of greasepaint that wafted over the auditorium the moment the curtain went up—all created pleasure and emotion, removing any sense of isolation.

They returned to Heath Edge at about six. There had been no messages, no telephone calls.

'A peaceful Sunday,' said Edward with approval. 'Marion and I have had a chance to talk for once, and we've done absolutely nothing except sit out on the patio—under the umbrellas, mark you. No roasting for me.'

'Or me,' Marion agreed. She looked from face to face, each bearing testimony to a state of happiness that was noticeable. Hester's arm was through Lance's as they stood together in the sitting room where they were now all gathered, Clive and Lydia having come in from the hammock.

Hester didn't want to move, but she knew she must relinquish her hold of Lance. As though attuned to her thoughts, he reached for her cane which was propped up against a nearby chair, and handed it to her.

'Thank you—for everything,' she smiled. 'You're a wonderful guide!'

It was, she thought, like saying goodbye, and her heart missed a beat. She dared not allow imagination to run riot and delude herself that there was anything beyond loving affection in Lance's feelings for her. It had never been more evident than that afternoon, when it would have been so easy for their inevitable proximity to have stimulated a furtive caress, emotion, rather than concern and tenderness, betrayed. She knew Lance well enough to appreciate that had he loved her, the fact that she was blind would not have proved any handicap from his point of view, merely deepened his love for her.

'I'm going to tidy up,' she said brightly. 'My hair must be on end, because we've had the car windows down so that I could hear and feel the wind.' She was very familiar with Heath Edge and moved confidently, hardly needing to use her cane until she got to the stairs.

Vivien followed her.

Lance smiled at Lydia before going from the room, 'You would have enjoyed the Copper Kettle; it was the real thing and not an artificial "olde-worlde" place.' He paused, and they both remembered that they had been there soon after they were married.

Edward said cheerfully, 'Don't forget we've got some champagne waiting.' He indicated a silver tray on which the glasses were already set out. 'We haven't forgotten someone's birthday, have we? Or some other occasion.'

Lance laughed. 'Nothing like that, I assure you.'

They all gathered some quarter of an hour later, and Edward brought in one of the bottles from the fridge. He handed it to Lance.

'It's your idea,' he laughed, 'to which we're not averse, so you open it.'

Lance wrapped the napkin around it so that it made the expert, barely audible sound, as he filled the glasses and handed them around.

Lydia tensed as she looked at him, for he was a man very much in command and, she thought, even pleased with himself as he moved to Vivien's side and said in his deep attractive voice, 'Vivien and I are getting married. . . I thought this was a good way to celebrate. I know we shall have all your good wishes.'

CHAPTER SIX

LYDIA heard Lance's announcement with shock and disbelief, the colour draining from her cheeks and the hand holding the glass trembling so that the contents were spilt. Her legs felt like cotton wool, her mouth was dry. She was aware of Hester's voice, tremulous behind the brave words of congratulation, and looked across the room at Lance. Their eyes met, their gaze holding for a split second, before she managed to say, 'I hope you'll both be very happy.' She knew that all eyes were upon her and that she must not betray her emotions.

'We've kept the secret pretty well, I think,' said Lance. 'But things were beginning to get a little difficult.'

'We even thought of slipping away and being married secretly.' Vivien spoke confidently.

'I'm glad you didn't.' Marion felt deflated, but added her good wishes. It seemed utterly ridiculous that Lance should be marrying Vivien when, in her, Marion's, eyes, Lydia was twice as attractive and had double the charm. Vivien was sophisticated, smart, but artificial by comparison; but no doubt, Marion argued, she knew how to flatter and cajole. The engagement endangered Marion's peace of mind and she hated the fact that her enthusiasm was forced and tinged with fear.

'And when,' asked Edward, sharing Marion's reactions, 'is the wedding to be?'

Vivien answered as they all sat down, she beside Lance on the sofa.

'Soon. . . we shall probably disappear one week-end and avoid any fuss.' She looked across at Lydia and added with deliberate insensitivity, 'And create a precedent.' She saw the faint frown that clouded Edward's face and hastened, 'It's so pleasant that we're all friends, and that there are no problems from the past to make me feel an intruder.' Inwardly she was vowing that Heath Edge was the one place from which she would keep away as much as possible once she was Lance's wife. She did not want Lydia in the picture and resented her friendship with Lance.

Lydia saw Lance alone for a few minutes before she and Clive left that evening.

'I hope everything will go well for you,' she said quietly.

'Thank you.'

'A well kept secret,' she added.

'That surprised you?' He was studying her intently.

'Yes; you've been very anti-marriage since we split up.' She knew she was exaggerating.

'Not really. *Cautious.* We have, after all, discussed the possibility of remarriage. And of your relation-ship with Clive.'

That was true, she thought despondently. Also, this event seemed to be the real divorce, not the previous legal severance. From now on Lance would have a fiancée and then a wife. The whole structure would inevitably change. Already she felt a little shy as though he had become a stranger, no longer in her world.

'How unprepared we are for tomorrow,' he said a little surprisingly. 'Things happen when we least expect them. We can sometimes be very blind.'

Vivien detached herself from Steven with whom she had been exchanging a few bantering words, and joined them, saying, 'You look very serious.' She slipped her arm through Lance's and glanced up at him enquiringly.

He smiled down at her.

'I was saying that we can sometimes be very blind,' he repeated.

'How true. I suppose Hester is the least blind of all in the things that matter.' Vivien felt triumphant. She had reached her goal. Lance could give her just the kind of life and security she wanted, was more than attractive and, to use her own terminology, 'madly in love with her'. The only disadvantage was Lydia, but she argued that the situation could be manoeuvred so that she disappeared from the scene. She would marry Clive and cease to work for Lance. It required only tact and manipulation to drive a wedge between the past and the present.

Clive, who had been congratulatory but somewhat subdued in the circumstances, walked up to Lydia—having said goodbye to the others—and said almost stiffly, 'If you're ready. . .' They were to have supper together at his house nearby.

'You're breaking up the party,' Vivien protested.

He glanced back at Steven, Hester, Edward and Marion, who were talking together.

'I'm quite sure you wouldn't mind if we all vanished!'

Lydia shot him an uneasy glance. There was something tense about him; an austerity, foreign, which was out of tune with the occasion.

Lance laughed. 'It's you and Lydia who are doing the vanishing act, but we understand!'

The only words drumming in Lydia's brain were, *'Lance is in love with Vivien and going to marry her.'*

It seemed part of a fantasy. She wanted to get away from the house, the atmosphere, and Vivien's self-satisfied, possessive happiness.

Marion said, when Lydia kissed her goodbye, 'Keep in touch. Don't let this make any difference to *us*. . . I'd miss you, Lydia,' she added in a whisper. 'Never forget that. Edward, too. To us, you'll always be part of the family.'

Lydia choked back the tears and was grateful when she and Clive drove away in their respective cars, to Clive's comfortable Victorian house. They settled in the spacious chintzy and friendly sitting room, and he said somewhat belligerently, his mood baffling Lydia. 'I'm very glad Lance has found happiness at last. While one wondered about Vivien, it was still a closely guarded secret. . . You look pale and solemn.'

Lydia struggled to be natural, but her voice lacked strength and her smile was false.

There was a long, unnerving silence before she exclaimed anxiously, 'Clive, what's wrong? You—'

'I've learned the truth today,' he said, suddenly quiet. 'I know why you've hesitated about marrying me.'

Lydia felt that the walls of the high-ceilinged room were leaning down, suffocating her. She managed to say breathlessly, 'I don't follow—'

Clive's voice was low and impressive as he cut in, 'You're in love with him—you're in love with your ex-husband, whether you realise it or not.'

Lydia was shocked. She stared at him, at first angrily, accusingly, then with bewilderment.

'What *are* you talking about. . . really, Clive—' But she was trembling; emotion was surging over her reaching every pore and sinew until it seemed she was lost in a world of ecstasy, desire and truth which stripped her of pretence, and mocked her futile efforts to deny that which had struck like lightning when she had heard that Lance was to be married. And in that moment of revelation she became very still; her acceptance almost a relief as she said on the note of a deep sigh, 'Yes, Clive; I do realise it, but I've only accepted it at this moment.' She held his gaze appealingly. 'How did you guess, I mean—'

'Your expression when Lance made that announcement. You were white. Everyone else was watching Lance and Vivien; only *I* watched *you*.'

Colour rose in her cheeks. If she were asked if she had, unknowingly, loved Lance all along, or had just fallen in love with him, she wouldn't have been able to give a truthful answer. He had sexually attracted her during these past months and she had dismissed the fact as representative of no more than propinquity and circumstances, dissociated from serious love.

She added with genuine concern, 'If I'd realised I'd have been honest with you, Clive—told you that there was someone else.' Her voice was quiet and sincere. 'I wanted to agree to marry you. The idea of working with you and Edward appealed to me enormously, and yet something held me back. I couldn't understand it myself, because you mean a very great deal to me and I'd hate you to go out of my life.'

His anger, hurt, disappointment had subsided and he knew he could not contemplate living without her.

'You won't lose me,' he said firmly. 'I know you didn't deliberately deceive me. In fact,' he added wryly, 'when it comes to it we're in the same boat—in love with people who don't love us.'

Put into words, the truth stung, and Lydia cried inside because once she had been Lance's *wife*. There couldn't be anything more ironical than to fall in love with her divorced husband; or more hopeless, since he was to marry another woman.

Lance's words re-echoed, *'How unprepared we are for tomorrow. Things happen when we least expect them. We can sometimes be very blind.'*

'Love,' said Clive, 'is unfathomable and plays havoc with all rational thought. Tomorrow is a frighteningly unknown factor.'

'Lance said we were unprepared for it.'

'Implying that his love for Vivien had an element of shock. . . Edward will be very disappointed about your not joining us,' he added irrelevantly. 'Although we hadn't gone into any details about the possibility, I know the idea delighted him.'

Lydia felt sad. She did not want the loneliness of being in love with Lance, or the upheaval it would make in her life.

Clive said suddenly and a little dramatically, 'People have been known to get over one love by encouraging another. It's unthinkable that you should spend the rest of your life alone.'

She looked amazed.

'Meaning that you still want to marry me?' Her voice held astonishment.

'Had you asked me that question when I first realised your feelings for Lance, my answer would have been a definite "no"; but reason having prevailed, yes; yes, I would take that risk. There's nothing so dead as a dead love, and you're not the type of woman to spend the rest of her life being faithful to an unrequited passion.' Clive had calmed down and was consoling himself with philosophies which might or might not be valid.

'I don't know what type of woman I am,' said Lydia a little belligerently. 'At the moment I feel extremely foolish and vulnerable because you know. It isn't the kind of secret one wants to betray.'

'I shan't give up,' he warned her. 'There's no guarantee with love, although we foster that illusion. Will you promise me that if you feel you *could* marry me, even allowing for your feelings at the moment, you'd be honest and tell me? We could build a life together, Lydia; we already have more in common than many married people.'

She looked at him with obvious affection. 'I could make you that promise, but it wouldn't be fair to you.'

'Let me be the judge of that,' he said firmly.

At that moment Lydia would have liked the oasis of that solid house and the security of Clive's love, instead of the upheaval, physical as well as mental, she was now enduring.

When, later, she returned to her flat it seemed to be denuded of all its furniture. It was the home she and Lance had created together and where, before, she had accepted the fact, now everything had a new significance. Once he had been there with her. She must have been mad, she told herself, to have agreed to a divorce on what seemed, now, such a flimsy pretext as incompatibility and the breakdown of the marriage. She'd been like a child who had grown tired of a toy and discarded it—just as he had. Now she ached to have it back; she wanted him there in her arms, to lie with him in that bed and make love until there was no light left in the sky. And he was going to marry Vivien whom she could not honestly say she even liked. How long would her own friendship with Lance survive? And how soon would he want her to leave?

Clive telephoned her just as she was getting into bed.

'You'll be feeling low and unhappy,' he said, his voice soothing. 'But don't forget there are many kinds of love and that I'm always here.'

Tears were running down Lydia's face as she replaced the receiver.

Mrs Trent, Nurse Webster and Julie shot each other surreptitious and surprised glances when Vivien told them the news on her way in to see Lance the following morning. Una Mercer, the health visitor, who had just arrived, overheard as she walked into Mrs Trent's office.

'Engaged!' they exclaimed, almost in chorus, without knowing why the fact should be such a shock, since Doctor Richmond and Miss Wayne had seemed far more friendly recently.

'We've surprised everyone,' Vivien said complacently, giving them all a beaming smile, then she made sure from Mrs Trent that it was in order to see Lance and hurried to his room. It was early and the building was only just beginning to come to life.

'Darling,' she whispered as she went straight to his arms, 'I've told them, and Una Mercer was there.'

'I've got to have a word with Lydia before we begin surgery. . .' He kissed her and stood back, feeling a little awkward. 'You manage to make even a white coat look smart,' he said honestly.

'Everything went off very well yesterday.' Vivien wanted to reminisce. 'It must have been strange for Lydia—but she took it in her stride.'

'Of course,' he said, as though anything less was unthinkable. 'Vivien,' he added half-apologetically, 'I must get to work—it's one hell of a day. This evening, I hope.'

'I'll get a cold supper,' she said immediately. 'My three-times-a-week lady comes this morning, so I was able to leave the chores.'

He nodded, switched on the intercom and asked Mrs Trent to tell Lydia that he was free.

Vivien hovered until Lydia came into the room, then, with complacency, went out.

Lydia struggled to be natural, to ignore Lance, the man, and concentrate purely on their professional relationship. He looked at her directly for a second, seemed about to say something, and then a second later exclaimed, 'I've got a case I want you to see—a new patient, Miss Morgan, transferring from Doctor White. We'll discuss it when you're in the picture. A girl of twenty or so. Problems.'

'Always problems,' Lydia said with a sigh.

'You'll solve them: you have the knack.'

She thought how grateful she would be to solve her own. There was something in the atmosphere, as though they were two amateurs trying to avoid each other on an ice rink. His praise was welcome, but she was tongue-tied and struggling not to betray her nervousness and emotion.

He said suddenly and urgently, 'We shall have to talk, Lydia.'

A sick sensation churned in the pit of her stomach.

'Yes,' she agreed, unable to concentrate fully on anything when all she could think of was that he had been her *husband*.

The intercom went. Surgery was about to begin.

Lydia saw Miss Morgan that afternoon. She never allowed herself any preconceived notions about patients, but she was not prepared for the white skeleton who came in and sat down. Her dark eyes were sunk in their sockets, her cheekbones stood out; she had the figure of a starved boy. She was twenty-three.

'I keep losing weight,' she said in a thin, rather frightened voice. 'Doctor White didn't under-stand—no one understands. I've been to a psychiatrist, but it was all nonsense. I've had an awful job to get here without my mother coming too. Rel-atives won't leave you alone!'

'Would you expect them to when you're starving yourself to death?' Lydia said boldly.

Normally Crissie Morgan was beautiful, with an oval, almost Spanish type of beauty; now she looked an old woman, her hands claw-like as they clenched themselves in her lap. She gave a cry of resentment and denial.

'I came to you for help, not to be—be *accused!*'

'I can only help you by dealing with the truth,' Lydia said with a quiet firmness. 'Let me go over you and see how you really are.'

'I'm fat,' came the resentful exclamation. 'I hate being fat.'

'Then suppose we weigh you first.'

'I don't want to be weighed.' There was a petulant resistance in the utterance. 'I'm tired of weighing so much.' She hurried on, 'I lost my boy-friend because of that.'

Lydia glanced down at the case-notes which had been passed on by her previous doctor in which he spoke of psychological problems which no amount of psychiatry had succeeded in treating successfully. She was an hysterical personality. Lydia didn't pur-sue the question of weight, because she judged it to be under six stone.

'But,' she shot at her, 'you don't eat very much to make yourself so fat.'

A half-suspicious glance came with the comment, 'My family are always pestering me to eat. You'd think I'm half-starved to hear them!'

'Starvation can lead to death,' Lydia suggested, watching her carefully.

'So what? Looking as I do, what is there to live for?' She went on, 'And it's no good sending me to another psychiatrist. They're crazy people—ask the most stupid questions. Treat you as though you were some nut case! I came to you to get away from all that. I thought you'd be different. Doctor White hadn't any patience with me.'

Doctor White had Lydia's sympathy as she said, deliberately staring Crissie Morgan out, 'Actually, Miss Morgan, you eat a very great deal—far more than is good for you.'

'I eat normally.' The words came on a note of protest.

Lydia ignored that as she said, 'You can lie to me—that isn't important. People do that a great deal of the time. . . it's when you lie to *yourself* that the trouble starts. . . You eat secretly and then, because you're afraid of getting fat, you make yourself sick; you take purgatives. You have multiple vitamin and mineral deficiencies—'

A cry of frustration, fear and anger rang through the room, 'You know nothing about me! You—'

'And your periods have ceased.'

In truth the effects of anorexia nervosa included changes in endocrine gland function—the pituitary, adrenal, thyroid and the sex glands—and was responsible for depression and hysteria. Lydia knew she was dealing with an extreme case which, if not rescued from starvation, would die.

That remark struck a chord that brought a response.

'You're right about that!'

'I'm right about it all, Miss Morgan, and because I'm probably repeating what you've already been told, it doesn't make it any the less true.' Lydia paused and added gravely, 'It's only when you face up to that truth that we can begin to cure you. I can't give you any magic antibiotic, or medicine, that will take the place of will power and enable you to see what you're doing to yourself.'

'I want to improve my figure.' It was the statement of a child demanding a toy.

'You mean you want to regain it,' Lydia corrected. 'Do you think it attractive to look like a starving little boy? You've lost your breasts, but they'll come back once you begin to eat and live normally. If you keep to the diet I shall give you, I can promise that you'll look beautiful, and as slim as you could ever wish to be. It's up to you. Only don't waste my time by telling me things that my intelligence can't accept. I've got sick people to see; not those who make *themselves* sick.'

Crissie Morgan recoiled as though struck. She had been shaken out of her self-pity, her weakness in believing that she was the victim of some complaint over which she had no control. Like the alcoholic, she could not be cured unless she admitted the curse and craved to be free of it. And Lydia rightly judged that the stage of sympathy and cajoling, of expert psychiatry, was over. If this jolt didn't contribute to her recovery, she doubted if anything else would. Doctor White might already have tried it, but a second challenge would not be amiss in any case. She watched the emaciated face carefully, saw the annoyance, defiance and anger that distorted it in a few moments of tense and bitter silence, before Crissie crumpled up and said, 'At this minute I know you're right. If only I could accept it all the time!'

'You will if you want to enough. Think of your parents and all they must have gone through—*are* going through. Is it fair to drag them into all this? And if you want any kind of normal life in the future, this behaviour must stop. Do you understand? Not even a doctor can tell you the repercussions later on, if you don't return to a normal way of eating.'

'And if—if I do as you say?' For the first time a look of hope crept into the hollow-cheeked face.

'You'll get back to normal and be well again.'

'Anorexics relapse.'

Lydia could not contradict her, because in many cases the basic psychological problem remained.

'We shall have to make sure that you don't,' she suggested. 'Think of the joy to your family.'

'My mother used to talk to Doctor White. I don't want her talking to you. . . She went to him before I saw him. I'm never sure how much she knows—'

'No facts about a patient's case are ever divulged without his or her consent, but I'm quite sure that without being told your mother knows your problem and quite naturally, and rightly, consulted Doctor White.'

'If I had your diet sheet she'd be satisfied that something was being done.' There was a note of contrition as Crissie added, 'She's very good really; I've given her a bad time. . . I'll try, Doctor Richmond.'

'Splendid! Now, I'd like to examine you, reassure myself. I don't treat patients without that protection—'

'You'll have my notes from Doctor White with all the details,' came the swift reply.

'I make my own judgements,' Lydia said warningly, realising that while Miss Morgan was a skeleton and physically weak, there was nothing wrong with her mental reactions—a fact which comforted her.

After the examination, Lydia was satisfied that the degeneration was not at such a serious level that hospitalisation was necessary. A balanced diet was the only treatment needed.

'I shall want to see you every week,' she said with encouragement.

'You can't do much in a week.'

'You'd be surprised what proper food, no vomiting or purgatives, can achieve in seven days,' Lydia replied. 'I don't expect miracles, but when you're better it will seem like one.'

'You've been very patient and understanding. And honest with me. None of this moralizing. I'll try not to let you down,' Crissie promised.

'I'm sure you will.'

'And I can tell my mother that I need this particular diet to—to give me an appetite?'

'Yes.' Lydia knew the mother would not be deceived, only thankful to clutch at any fresh hope. Anorexia nervosa did not only devastate the sufferer, but those around them.

The skeleton-like figure dragged herself from the room.

Lance listened intently as, over a cup of tea drunk in the common room, Lydia outlined what had happened. He looked and seemed pleased.

'Just the right approach,' he said appreciatively. 'I like that phrase about not lying to herself. We could all learn something from those words. . . By the way, did you get an invitation to Toby's christening this morning?'

'Yes. I was thrilled.' Lydia was thankful to keep the conversation going so that she could avoid any silence when his eyes met hers, and was terrified of betraying her feelings.

'Elsa Martin is a different woman—much better; the heart has stood up to it all amazingly well. . . I got an invitation, too. That's one thing we must manage to go to. It's a Sunday, thank God.'

As is often the case in moments of tension, Lydia said the wrong thing.

'The Martins won't, of course, know about your engagement, otherwise they wouldn't have asked us both.'

Lance stared at her as though she were mad.

'What on earth has that to do with it? Because I'm going to marry again, it doesn't mean I mustn't be seen in public with you. I never heard such nonsense!'

'Vivien has—'

'Vivien accepts our relationship as everyone else does,' he said loftily, then paused, holding her gaze with a deep enquiry. 'Or is it that *you* feel differently about it all?'

Lydia felt her heartbeats must be audible. Emotion was overwhelming her as she looked into his dark compelling eyes and she felt that every nerve in her body was sensitised in her love and desire for him.

'Well?' he demanded. 'Do you?' He made it sound as though he would consider it outrageous were she to say yes.

She hastened on, not daring to risk a scene, 'No; no, of course not. I was thinking of Vivien.'

'Then let me do that, and decide what I shall or shall not do,' he demanded. 'We shall go to that christening together.' A devastating appealing smile touched his faintly humorous mouth. 'Don't forget we're still professional colleagues.'

Lydia stood there, shaken, realising that he was blind to any complications. The door of the past slammed in her face.

'Of course. . . you did say we must talk?' she reminded him, trying to keep her voice even.

'So much seems to be crowding in. I didn't realise getting engaged meant quite such an upheaval. . . I seem to remember that we went about it very quietly.'

'I hadn't any parents to make it a celebration, which, in view of all that's happened, was as well. . .'

He said immediately, 'Vivien wants a restaurant party. I'm glad—it will spare Marion the extra work.'

Passion, a natural jealousy and hurt, made Lydia say, forcing a note of lightness into her voice, 'At least you won't expect me to be *there*.'

'Oh, yes, I shall. It wouldn't be right without you and Clive.'

For a second there was a tense, almost electric silence before she said quietly, 'I'm not going to marry Clive. This is as good a time as any to tell you. I shan't be joining the practice after all.'

CHAPTER SEVEN

LANCE'S expression was one of amazement as he heard Lydia's words. He had taken Clive's part in her life very much for granted, seeing their eventual marriage as a foregone conclusion, while believing, as he had previously said, that Clive was the right man for her and would make her happy.

'Your turn for surprises,' he said, looking at her earnestly. 'I'm sorry; the whole idea seemed ideal.' He paused as Nurse Webster came into the room, telling them that their respective patients had arrived.

Lance looked slightly vague, hesitated, and then said almost solemnly to Lydia, 'We'll soon have to make an appointment really to talk.' He was already on his way out of the room, Lydia following to see Trudy Hall, who was now looking the dark-haired pretty woman Lydia had first known. She came straight to the point.

'Neville wants us to have a holiday in Rome. He's never liked travelling and doesn't even like going out. But,' she hastened, 'it's months since he was violent—you remember the last time I rushed here?'

'Only too well.'

'I couldn't rush to Dr Richard or you from Rome,' came the revealing remark. 'on the other hand, if I thwart him in this, spoil his pleasure, might it not trigger off the very thing I fear?' She lowered her gaze for a second and then looked at Lydia directly, 'I told my myself I'd lost that fear, but I realise it's the familiarity of the routine that enables me to keep on some kind of even keel and put the past behind me. In unfamiliar circumstances I have no yardstick with which to measure his behaviour. Holiday travelling. . . one has no guarantee of times. There are bound to be delays at some point. . . I would have been willing to stay at home for the rest of my life if he were content,' she added.

Lydia said with conviction, 'I'm afraid it's a risk you'll have to take. Do you personally want to go? Just think of yourself for a moment—something you never do!'

The words came spontaneously, 'Oh, I'd love it! I've always wanted to see Rome.'

'Then this is probably his way of atonement for all the misery he's caused you, and all the things he's denied you—in every direction.'

'You've no idea how good he is to me now,' Trudy Hall said earnestly, and with a loyalty that was one of her finest characteristics.

Lydia felt she had to unlock the prison gates as she said, 'Then have that holiday. Don't forget he would be under a certain restraint in a foreign country and be afraid to risk any trouble,' she added quietly. 'I think your staying out for some hours after he was violent the last time scared him. You could do the same thing again, and in a foreign country—well, he wouldn't risk being left alone.'

'You're such a comfort Dr Richmond. And what you say is so very true.'

When Trudy Hall left the building she was already mentally packing for the trip.

Meanwhile Hester had remained at Heath Edge. Bunty had gone to see an invalid aunt, and while Hester often stayed alone at the flat, Marion was never happy about it and loved her company. This evening was different for them all; the normal bright conversation and happy atmosphere were missing. The August evening reflected their mood, for it was chilly and had a touch of autumn in the air as the light began to fade. Hester sat facing the large sitting-room windows which overlooked the Heath, and into the far distance where the London skyline was a blaze of light; even in the gloom, it had a magnificence like that of a tapestry woven into the sky.

Hester's heart ached; she felt empty and sad. She had never dared to allow herself to think that Lance might return her love, but she had dreamed of his doing so, and in those moments touched Paradise. She could have borne his engagement to Vivien more easily if she felt it was for his happiness, or if she could like her and escape from an instinctive distrust. It seemed that a priceless ornament had been shattered and the broken pieces scattered around her. Nothing would be the same again and, in her world, emotional security was a star. She had always felt free with Lance, even when he was married to Lydia. There were no restraints except those she was forced to impose on herself because of her feelings for him.

She sat there, very still, when Marion moved across to her, putting out a hand and clasping hers before sitting down in a chair next to hers. It was an instinctive gesture, and a protective one.

'I'm frightened, Marion.' The words came solemnly. 'I can talk to you.'

'Frightened?' Marion echoed the word which struck a responsive chord.

'That everything will be changed. Nothing will be the same,' added Hester, her voice shaken. 'Heath Edge has been such a wonderful place; you've made it home for us all.'

'It will still be that,' Marion assured her without believing it. 'I've already told Lydia we should miss her very much if she didn't come here as usual, and there's no question of it making any difference where you're concerned.' She uttered the words deliberately while knowing them to be a forlorn hope, since Hester was in love with Lance. Now Hester's emotions were intensified by her blindness. Unrequited love was commonplace: Hester's lay in the shadow of near-tragedy.

There were tears in Hester's sightless eyed as she murmured, 'Vivien won't want—' She stopped. 'But I mustn't let my imagination run away with me. I thought, for a little while, that she was being very kind to me. . . I'd better try to believe that. It's so easy to be unfair.'

'I know,' Marion sighed.

'Talking helps,' Hester said quietly. 'Knowing a person understands.' She turned her face to Marion's and said with a touching simplicity, 'I love Lance; I always have.' She gave a sigh that relieved pain. 'I never thought I would actually utter those words to anyone, but you're his mother and very special.'

'Dear Hester!' Marion's hand closed over hers. 'All you want is his happiness, as I do.'

There was a second of deep silence. The echo of those words, 'I love Lance', seemed to float on the air like music, uplifting consoling, bringing the message that love was never wasted, and beautified all it touched.

At that moment Edward came into the unlit room and said, 'You can't sit here in the dark.'

The tension broke as Hester laughed, 'Dear Edward, I'm always the dark! Someone met me in the

street one winter's evening and said, "You ought not
to be in the dark"! It was quite funny, but they were
concerned.' She laughed and for a split second the
pain eased. She thanked God that she had Edward
and Marion. They were Lance's parents. . . Through
them, he would always be close to her.

Lance was delayed by a bronchitis patient on his way
to Vivien that evening, having telephoned that he
would be late.

'I don't know why I've agreed to marry a doctor,'
she said in greeting. 'Unreliable people who can never
be on time.'

'I'm glad you used the words "can never", because
they haven't a clue themselves what they're likely to
be doing.'

Her arms went around his neck and he held her for
a second before going into the sitting room which he
had never really studied. Vivien had come into his life
rather like a whirlwind after a period of friendship
and he realised, as he looked around him, that the
surroundings were somewhat bizarre, their modern-
ity with black and tangerine furnishings smart, but
nothing to which he had been accustomed. Vivien
rented the flat on a lease which was coming to an end
and she had it in mind for Lance to buy a large flat—
his didn't appeal to her, any more than she liked his
housekeeper. If it meant his moving further away
from Carisbrooke and involving a journey, so be it.
She had every intention of giving up her job once she
was married, for, although she had never confessed
it to anyone, she did not like her position as assistant
to Susan Rengold who ran the physiotherapy unit.
She hadn't the money to start on her own, and
resented being subordinate at no matter what level.
Her parents, by no means affluent, were divorced,

and she didn't like either of them, so they seldom met. On the other hand she knew, from Steven, that Lance had a private income, left to him by a paternal aunt. It was in no way a secret, but Lance had not mentioned it since financial matters had never been discussed.

'I thought you might like a Chinese meal,' she said a few minutes later, as they went into the small dining room where a scarlet tablecloth and white napkins produced a striking effect. 'It will be fun discovering each other's likes and dislikes. Strange how you discover people suddenly after just seeing them for years.'

Lance was thinking that he was not over-fond of Chinese food, but was prepared to get to like it; and as for discovering people, he exclaimed guardedly, 'Do we ever really discover the truth about anyone? It strikes me that we're all mysteries.'

'It could be very boring to know anyone too well,' she said provocatively. 'But one thing I *do* know about you!' She held his gaze, a tantalising smile on her lips.

'And that?'

'You're a very attractive, fascinating man. . . but I'm sure many women have told you that.' She used the plural, but wondered if Lydia had ever done so.

'On the contrary.' Lance looked embarrassed. He could not embark on a series of compliments to her, because he believed they should always be spontaneous.

'Lance?' The utterance of his name held significance.

'Yes?' He was instantly alert.

'Would you mind if I were an old-fashioned wife?'

'That's a leading question! It depends on what you mean by old-fashioned.'

'I'd like to give up work; be at home and have a family.'

He looked amazed. 'Are you serious?'

'Perfectly. I want a real home; somewhere you can come back to and find me there—oh, not in a dreary sense; heaven forbid!' Vivien put a hand out across the table and took his. 'Not two people both weary at the end of the day; never having time to discuss things, or even *do* things together.' She watched him carefully, knowing she was saying all the right things.

'Then I couldn't be more pleased,' he said honestly. 'Oh, I've nothing,' he added frankly, 'against people both working, but if they want a family and it can be arranged to begin with, at least—' He stopped because it was painful to seem to be denigrating the pattern of his and Lydia's life.

She said innocently, 'Of course, if it were a matter of financial necessity—that's different. I'd—'

'There's no question of that!' he said firmly.

'Ah!' she said with a contented sigh. 'You want children?'

As she spoke, she saw children as part of the scene, with a nanny in charge.

'Yes.' He didn't hesitate.

'I'll try to make it a boy and a girl.'

He stared at her a little bewildered. It was not the kind of conversation he had expected, but he knew, deep within him, that he wanted the security of home life; the life that had been enjoyed at Heath Edge and which he and Lydia seemed to have missed by avoidance, rather than any definite design. Now he was tired of living alone; of the emptiness of silent rooms and a solitary bed. He wanted a marriage as he had once envisaged it, and hoped he might find it with Vivien. She was vital, flatteringly in love with him, and now, asking *him* if he would like to share the same pattern. It seemed too good to be true.

But in that second a shadow crept over him as he thought of Lydia. He no longer had the peace of mind of knowing her happiness and future were secure, and that she would be working with Edward.

Vivien exclaimed with faint apprehension, 'You look very solemn all of a sudden!'

He felt that he was coming out of a trance without knowing the reason. It was foolish to have preconceived notions about Lydia's life. Nevertheless, he was curious as to the reason for her unexpected decision about Clive. Had she met someone else? Impossible. He himself would have known. Yet, he argued, why should he—any more than she had known all the facts about him and Vivien?

'I appreciate everything you've just said,' he assured her.

She raised her glass of Chablis.

'To us,' she smiled.

They drank.

How many times, Lance thought, had those words been said; and did the repetition devalue them? How many times could one love and recapture passion, ecstasy and excitement? He recalled once saying to Lydia that he and she had been sexually incompatible, but on reflection it seemed a far too strong and even facile, assessment, particularly in view of the kiss they had exchanged. . .

He looked at Vivien with a new interest. He was going to marry her—this elegant, sophisticated girl sitting beside him. He felt his heart thudding almost with fear. This was for life. He had a sensation as though some part of him had gone on ahead and he was searching for it in unfamiliar territory. Emotion

was churning within him without bringing any relief
from tension. The scene around him dissolved into
nothingness and he found himself at a loss for words.
Abruptly he put out his hand and clasped hers like a
man searching for salvation, willing a happiness he
had been craving for months, trying to sink into the
comfort of having found it.

Vivien held his hand to her cheek and looked at
him with adoration that gave him confidence. But
everything said had significance, and the relaxed
conversations he was accustomed to having with
Lydia and Hester seemed far removed from a certain
drama that hung in the air during a sudden silence.
Lance was at a loss for words which the situation
demanded, and he consoled himself that the mere fact
of a sudden emotional relationship didn't automatically enable two people to establish an
understanding. Vivien was different from any other
woman he had ever met, becoming almost a challenge which had plunged him into an unpremeditated
engagement which, on reflection, he found astonish-
ing.

She said gently and with telling accuracy, 'You're
a very lonely man, Lance. Shall I ever be allowed into
your private world?'

He retrieved his hand from hers, her perception
disturbing.

'You're being fanciful,' he suggested evasively. 'I
doubt if there's any human being who doesn't know
loneliness sometimes.'

She plunged deliberately, 'I can understand that
an unhappy marriage must leave scars and
regrets. . . I'd like to think I can atone for the dis-
appointments and disillusionments.'

Lance felt he was listening to beautiful music
played in the wrong key.

'Lydia and I have not dwelt on that phase, or allowed it to jeopardise our friendship.' His voice was strong and held a note of warning of which he was unaware. 'Dwelling on the past—'

Vivien cut in with half-apologetic anxiety, 'I'm sorry. I expressed myself badly, but with all good intentions.' She hurried on, 'We have the future as well as today, and that's all that matters, darling.'

He brightened, feeling a little churlish as he endeavoured to sit in her chair. An ex-wife in the picture, even on a professional basis, could not be easy to accept. It was a problem with which he had to grapple, and the thought dismayed him. He wanted to lose himself in this new relationship and to feel an urgency for its fulfilment. He was a singularly fortunate man to have found a woman prepared to build her life around his. The problems would be solved, and in the meantime he had tomorrow to walk towards with confidence, and the conviction that Vivien had come into his life at just the right moment: the moment when he had the greatest need of her.

In the sitting room over coffee, Vivien tentatively brought up the subject of where they would live, taking it for granted that they would buy a property of some kind, and leaving it open for him to make suggestions. He was not very forthcoming, and she said casually, 'Would you ever consider moving out of Central London?' Her voice was soft and held a note of persuasion.

'Meaning,' he said immediately, 'that you would like to?'

'That's answering a question by asking another,' she retorted with a smile.

'Would you like a weekend place in the country?' He looked at her intently.

'Yes,' she replied swiftly, 'provided it wasn't too far out. There's the traffic to consider today.'

'The nearer to London the greater the congestion,' he pointed out. 'You have to go some distance before you can really get peace.'

'You've made Heath Edge your "country",' she suggested.

'It's secluded and seems very much a world of its own. It's been easy to—well, to escape there. It seems another world.'

'I can't say I'd like to live in Hampstead.' Vivien tried to keep the edge from her voice.

'Good heavens, I wasn't thinking of that. . . it would be absurd!'

She didn't want to precipitate matters by bringing Lydia into the picture and emphasising that she had no intention of living in the shadow of the past, but Lance said with understanding, 'We want new ground; a new pattern and a new life. Don't think I've overlooked that.'

'Thank you,' she said with a telling and calculated simplicity.

Later, when the curtains were drawn, two lamps gave a glowing romantic light. Vivien moved to sit beside Lance on the sofa where he had looked a little isolated, and met his gaze before sliding into his arms and kissing him deeply, passionately, conscious of a certain restraint, although he held her with an almost desperate roughness which was impossible rightly to interpret. He gave the uneasy impression that it was time for him to go.

She pressed hard against him, raising her eyes significantly to his.

'Stay, my darling,' she whispered, and there was no mistaking her meaning. 'I love you so much, want you—'

The silence was almost electric before he released her gently from his grasp and said with quiet firmness, 'No, Vivien; that isn't the picture as I see it. I don't want to be your lover.' The words came out involuntarily and he didn't realise their impact, or intend them to be hurtful, but the shock of her expression upset him and he hastened with a swift, almost shaken apology, 'Isn't the fact that I prefer a wife—'

She managed to conceal her anger as she cut in, 'I'm sure you mean it as a compliment. . . I'm sorry I didn't realise you were so conventional.' There was a faint cynicism in her voice as she added, 'Quite refreshing in these days.'

Lance had risen to his feet and stood there, feeling a prig, unable to fathom why it seemed all wrong to stay.

'Convention doesn't come into it,' he insisted.

She could not keep back the question, 'Then lack of desire?'

He protested strongly.

Vivien appreciated that she would lose face if she stressed the matter; they were on delicate ground. Perhaps he and Lydia had been lovers before they married and he did not want history to repeat itself.

'Then,' she said softly, 'I must let you go gracefully and not make the same mistake twice.'

Lance felt that any further remark on his part would make matters worse. All he knew was that he wanted this relationship to be uncomplicated and without pretence.

When they reached the front door she said, 'Are you sure you haven't changed your mind about marrying me?' She trembled with fear as she dared to ask the question.

'Oh, Vivien!' It was an indulgent reproach. 'Do I have to sleep with you to convince you that I want to marry you?'

She changed the mood deliberately. 'I've been awfully silly . . .'

'Just woman-like,' teased Lance without being at ease. He stooped and kissed her. 'We'll fix the date,' he said firmly.

He walked back to his flat and let himself into the square hall and so to the glass-doored sitting room, where he poured himself out a brandy from the decanter on the tray. The traffic was barely audible as he pulled back the curtains which Mrs Carson had drawn and looked across to Hyde Park, cool and mysterious under a full moon. What was he doing there alone, when he could have been lying in Vivien's arms? Since he wanted to marry her, why the reticence? Was it that the failure of divorce had set a new standard, made him superstitious about anticipating fulfilment? He didn't know, but sat down restlessly and held the glass on the arm of his chair, looking down into its contents for inspiration. He found that his thoughts did not seem to get beyond Clive and Lydia, and the problems that lay ahead so far as her connection with his, Lance's, practice was concerned. Emotional trauma set his nerves tingling and a strange sensation churning in the pit of his stomach. The telephone rang and he felt a sense of relief. An emergency would almost be welcome. But it was Vivien.

'No emergency,' she hailed him. 'Just checking to make sure you didn't walk into a bus. . .'

He felt a little awkward, and plunged without collecting his thoughts.

'How do you feel about marrying me early in the New Year?' He spoke urgently.

Vivien had thought of it being sooner, but she played for safety. 'I'd be delighted, provided you take me to the sun for our honeymoon.'

'Splendid idea.'

'Lance?'

'Yes?' He wondered what was coming.

'You were quite right. . . It will be rather special this way—different. I haven't been married, but I did have a boy-friend. He's married now. I don't know why I'm telling you this over the telephone. But I doubt if you imagined that I'd not had any experience.'

Actually, Lance had not questioned the fact, but he said honestly, 'If I'd dwelt on it I certainly should have assumed that an attractive woman like you. . .' His voice trailed away. 'It makes things more even. And I like your idea of a cottage in the country,' he went on irrelevantly, gaining enthusiasm as he talked.

'If my memory serves me rightly, you asked *me* about a place in the country?'

'But you asked me whether I would consider moving out of Central London.'

'We're being very meticulous,' she said with a laugh. 'But I'm glad you approve of the suggestion. After all, Steven finds his cottage near Ascot a great boon. We could do worse than look for something in that direction.'

'I always forget Steven has the place. He roams in and out of the picture without giving an account of himself.'

'A true bachelor,' she laughed.

Lance wondered if he himself, as a divorcé, was put in the same category. The idea didn't appeal to him. Perhaps, when it came to it, he *was* conventional at heart.

When Vivien eventually rang off, she immediately telephoned Steven.

He was instantly alert. 'Good heavens. . . something wrong?'

'Nothing . . . I want your help. You're the type to assist damsels in distress. It's about a cottage. I want Lance to buy a country place. You know everything about the district in which you live and it would be ideal if we could get somewhere there. Do you think you could produce one on the lines of, "There's an attractive property going near me"—you know what I mean? Be enthusiastic enough to stimulate his interest.'

'I haven't a clue if there's a property going in the area.'

'Well, within a radius. It's far enough out and has all the advantages.' She gave a little meaning laugh.

'I didn't think you'd find it easy to interest Lance in any weekend venture. He's too bound up with the life-style at Heath Edge.'

'You underestimate me.'

Steven made a significant sound. 'On the contrary. Property is like gold dust around here—'

'But you'll do what you can.'

'Which,' he said with sudden interest, 'reminds me, acquaintances of mine are selling up and going to the Bahamas. Their house is in Windsor. But that would be too simple.'

'I usually get my way,' Vivien said confidently. 'I'll ask you openly about it, or bring the subject up, at the party—that'll give you time between now and Saturday to collect all the facts. It isn't just a weekend place I have in mind, but an inducement for Lance to make changes, and get a junior partner who could take over on Lance's weekends off. Can't neglect the practice,' she added a trifle mockingly. 'Getting rid of Lydia is the main thing.'

'You don't miss a trick, do you?' His voice was faintly critical.

'No,' she said boldly. 'This is one hand I mean to win whatever happens.'

CHAPTER EIGHT

THE atmosphere at the practice that week was curiously flat. Mrs Trent's office was silent in those moments when Julie and Nurse Webster gathered for a momentary break between patients. They realised that Lance's engagement would inevitably change the pattern and that it was obvious Lydia would leave. If they thought she looked pale and subdued, no one mentioned the fact. It was a mark of respect, even affection.

Lance went into Lydia's room unexpectedly that Friday afternoon, before the engagement party on the Saturday, and threw himself down in the patients' chair. He looked weary and pale.

Lydia, surprised by his presence, exclaimed, 'Are you all right?'

He sighed, and his gaze sought her understanding.

'I've just come from delivering the Butterworth twins,' he said dully, 'and lost one. It lived only a matter of minutes.'

'Oh, no!'

'But the girl survived.'

'And they have a son already,' Lydia commented reflectively. 'I didn't realise you'd been called out.'

'She was a couple of weeks early and it was quick, but how I hate—' He didn't finish the sentence; it wasn't necessary. Losing a child was always doubly traumatic.

'You look as though you could do with a brandy,' Lydia suggested. 'And I don't like that cough.'

131

He ignored the reference to the cough and said, 'I have to go over to see old Mr Barnaby. . . this will be his last injection, I'm afraid. He's never got over his second coronary. But at ninety-one. . .' Lance looked affectionately indulgent. 'A great character—lived every minute of his life.' He got to his feet wearily, and again she asked him if he was all right, adding, 'You can't wilt tomorrow night, you know.'

He squared his shoulders, met her gaze and said as he walked to the door, 'How right you are.'

'Switch over to me this evening? I shall be in, and can deal with anything that comes through.'

'Are you sure? It's my turn.'

'Quite sure.'

'I should be grateful,' he admitted.

'Make an early night of it.'

He drew a hand across his forehead. 'Thanks, I will.'

He was almost in the corridor when he drew back over the threshold of the room.

'I forgot,' he said apologetically, 'I was going to *ask* you if you'd take the calls this evening. Vivien and I are going to a concert at the Barbican—it completely slipped my memory what with this afternoon's events. . . is it still all right?'

'Of course,' Lydia assured him, but the knife of jealousy stabbed her. 'You know my number if you need an emergency doctor!' With that she sat down at her desk and began to sign her letters. Lance went out quietly.

Lydia chose a pencil-slim black dress for the engagement party. It was delicately embroidered in diamanté at the neck and with a motif on the skirt, and showed off her slim figure—a figure Lance had always admired, she recalled, as she glanced at her

firm round breasts which the folds of the bodice subtly revealed. Her mood was grey and the taut nerves
in her stomach brought faint nausea every time she
dwelt on the facts. It was incongruous, she argued,
that she was even going to this celebration, but since
she and Lance had established their particular code
of conduct, to refuse to go would have invited con-
jecture, or introduced a sour note, to say nothing of
giving Vivien cause to accuse her of jealousy.
Acknowledging those facts didn't make the ordeal of
playing her part any easier. She would have everyone's support, she thought, which was ironical.
Edward, Marion, Hester, Clive and Steven—Steven,
who she felt suspected her feelings but was far too
sophisticated to betray the fact. It struck her that
Vivien had no one of her own family, or even a friend,
to support her, and while her excuses and reasons
were valid, it made her seem a solitary figure nevertheless.

Clive arrived, and exclaimed, 'My goodness! You
look terrific. The elegance of simplicity. . . I must say
this occasion is new even to me!'

'My ex-husband's fiancée,' Lydia said, deliberately stating the fact. 'Nothing today, when so many
divorcees are friendly. . . Far more civilised, too.'

Clive saw the pain behind the smile, and said
gently, 'You don't have to pretend to me.' He hurried on, not wanting to embarrass her, 'Hester's
coming, of course?'

'Nothing would be right without Hester. Bunty's
coming too.' Lydia was talking, but her thoughts
were with Lance. Would he remember how *they* had
cut out the celebrations, and went out alone to a quiet
candlelit dinner where they were not known, and how
Edward and Marion had understood? The excite-

ment, the promise . . . don't let me *think,* she prayed, for the tears, even then, stung her eyes. Dwell on patients; anything that was foreign to the festivities and their implications . . . Were Lance and Vivien lovers? Had Vivien already lain in his arms—?Lydia shivered and started like someone coming out of a trance. Better to get all the reminiscences over, end the self-torture and then let the champagne dull the misery so that she could come through the evening triumphantly. Vivien would be watching her, the situation no less intriguing in reverse.

They all met in the reception room of the Creswell Club, which had a fine view over St James's Park. Only Vivien was unfamiliar with it. A wide imposing staircase rose from the entrance, lit wth fine crystal chandeliers, the walls panelled in faint peach with gilt beading. Their feet sank into the thickly piled deep rose and cream embossed carpet. A magnificent portrait of the Queen hung over the impressive chimney piece, and vast floor-to-ceiling windows, curtained with sapphire velvet and deep gold-edged pelmets, gave elegance and grace. Flowers were massed in large vases placed on artistically arranged pedestals, and spacious armchairs and sofas offered the maximum of comfort.

Lydia's eyes met Lance's gaze in awareness. He stood out impressively in his dinner jacket, but she thought anxiously that he looked very unwell. The pallor had gone and his cheeks were flushed. But she told herself that it was a hot evening, although the room was cool and airy and the two massive French windows wide open, leading to a terrace and gardens.

Vivien said deliberately, but apparently without malice, 'Lydia, you have the advantage of knowing

No wonder it's used for family celebrations. . .
you're looking very charming,' she added.

Lydia murmured a quiet, 'Thank you,' adding,
'yes, this is a special club, and I'm sure you'll thoroughly enjoy it in the future.'

Steven, watching carefully, thought it was like the
prologue of a play and felt he was holding his breath
in anticipation of what was to come.

Hester turned her head in a circular movement to
include them all as they settled in their respective
chairs to receive the drinks. 'I can feel the atmosphere of the past whenever I come here, and see all
the famous people—actors, artists—walking through
these same rooms.' Whenever Hester spoke she had
a soothing effect, and she looked exquisite in cream
lace, with a little frill at the neck and a Victorian
cameo brooch to complete the picture. Her hair was
piled gracefully upon her head and the sunlight
streaked it with gold.

Edward and Marion were tense as Vivien held out
her hand to show off her emerald-and-diamond
engagement ring, letting Hester touch it so that she
could 'see' and express her admiration. Clive
remained quiet, and concentrated on Hester.

Lydia subconsciously looked down at her wedding ring, above which was an antique circle of rubies
which had belonged to her mother. Lance's rather
glassy eyes turned in her direction, his gaze lingering
for a second and then moving swiftly away.

It was when they had gone into the high-ceilinged
dining-room, with its polished tables and mats, and
the champagne had been served, that Vivien said
suddenly and confidentially, 'Has Lance—' She
turned to Edward and Marion—'Has,' she repeated,
'Lance mentioned that we're thinking of getting a
weekend cottage in the country?'

Steven seized his opportunity. 'Really? Are you serious?'

'Very. . . aren't we, darling?' Edward and Marion had not heard of the plan.

Lance was very still, his eyes half-closed, but he made a gesture of assent.

Steven went on smoothly, 'I might be able to help if you want a place within easy radius. Friends of mine are selling their house at Windsor and would reduce the price for a quick no-fuss sale. It isn't even in the agents' hands.'

Lance coughed—a hard, dry cough. He felt desperately ill. His head was thumping; he had pleural pain, a high temperature and rapid pulse, and knew he had been mad to believe he could put on an act and get through the evening when he should have been in bed. He was afraid his legs might not support him when he attempted to move.

It was Hester who cried in dismay, 'Lance isn't well!'

Edward and Marion exchanged alarmed glances, facing up to the fact they had both tried to ignore since first seeing him that evening.

Vivien said, '*Darling*—'

Lance managed to whisper . . . 'So sorry; afraid. . . not too good.'

Lydia felt sick with anxiety. Why hadn't she challenged him yesterday, said something tangible? And why were doctors so foolish when it came to their own ailments, indifferent to symptoms they would immediately have dealt with in their patients?

Edward got to his feet. 'We'll take you back to Heath Edge—'

Vivien said on a note of authority, 'I've had some nursing experience, and if—'

Lance made a supreme effort as he interrupted her, and there was an expression of authority on his flushed face. 'Ring Matron at St Luke's Nursing Home. No fuss; better there . . . for everyone's sake.' He finished weakly, 'I insist.'

Edward knew it was the wisest thing. Lance was too ill merely to be 'looked after'.

Clive strode from the table, murmuring, 'I'll get through.'

Steven went and stood with Edward beside Lance's chair, ready to help Lance out to a car. Vivien joined him, flashing a somewhat confident look in Lydia's direction, while inwardly seething. She had counted on this evening being a triumph, with the house issue settled and the pattern of their future established. As it was, she had an air of one who was tacitly in charge.

'I shall come along to see you later,' she whispered to Lance who, hanging on to Edward and Steven, dragged himself from the dining room and so to Edward's car, where he collapsed on the back seat.

Clive hurried towards them. 'I've spoken to Matron,' he said reassuringly. 'It's all laid on.' He got in beside Lance, and Edward instructed, talking to Steven through the open driving window, 'Take over.' He implied that he and Clive would be back when they had seen Lance into St Luke's.

And at the table, Lydia sat icy and distressed. Hester's hand crept into hers in sympathy and understanding. Lydia knew that Lance had an indomitable spirit, but she also knew that just then he was a very sick man, and her heart ached with fear and worry. She had no rights whatsoever when it came to making decisions on his behalf, and the knowledge stung.

Steven returned. Vivien looked suitably subdued and forlorn, glancing from face to face and saying,

'Lance would be very upset if something wasn't salvaged, and we've got to sort the cars out and get to our respective homes . . . I wish he hadn't chosen to go to St Luke's—'

'He was quite right,' Marion said firmly, her face pale. 'Whatever is wrong, they have the facilities, and the chances are he would have had to go there in the end.'

'I agree,' said Lydia, groaning inwardly, the longing to take care of him overwhelming.

Vivien persisted, 'If Lance only has 'flu, Mrs Carson and I—'

Steven exclaimed, almost warningly and with directness, 'Men are better patients in hospital than at home, and Mrs Carson isn't very sympathetic towards illness.'

Vivien sighed, and they lapsed into an awkward silence. Marion shrank from the thought of Lance marrying Vivien with whom she could not feel any sympathy. It would have been natural in the circumstances for this situation to have drawn them closer, but as it was, the gap had widened and she could not pretend to bridge it.

'Thank heaven for you,' she said suddenly to Lydia. 'Lance will be spared so much worry over the practice.'

'And I'm sure Edward and Clive will rally around,' Vivien put in significantly.

Hester dared not betray her feelings, but the silent bond between her and Marion eased the pain. At least she would be kept in the picture. Bunty remained discreetly silent after expressing her concern. She was aware of the drama around her and amazed that Lance should ever have chosen anyone like Miss Wayne, after having been married to Lydia . . .

Lance had bacterial pneumonia.

Lydia sat in the subdued light of his pleasant room at the nursing home, praying that the Penbritin would prevent any spread of the infection. He had escaped pleurisy. It was four days after the fateful night; his temperature was lower, his breathing easier, and he was sleeping peacefully. She had come in late, just to reassure herself, having seen him earlier in the day to acquaint him with the practice details and that it was ticking over with nothing more serious at the moment than summer ailments and the complaints of their regular patients. Clive had done an emergency appendectomy, and Una Mercer had visited several elderly patients who were Lydia's routine cases.

Now all was still. Night staff had taken over; the lights were dimmed and it was time for her to go. Nurse West looked in, saw Lydia, and smiled. The Richmond story made interesting conversation over a lull in the activities. For an ex-wife, whose ex-husband was engaged to another woman, Lydia was incredibly attentive, even allowing for the fact that she was his locum. It was an original twist on the familiar divorce theme.

'He's better,' said Lydia, as though she were begging an affirmative response.

'The Penbritin is working,' came the reassuring comment. 'When he came in, I thought we'd be doing cultures—the lot. . .' She paused for a second, then, 'You must be very tired.'

Lydia flushed. She was aware of her position and of the interest it must, of necessity, arouse. She was equally a woman in love, and the hurt was as deep as the fear. She got to her feet. Nurse West left.

Lydia stood looking down on Lance, whose breathing was more rhythmic. He didn't stir and she thanked God that his pulse and respiration were creeping back to normal. She had read his chart, and while she realised he had some way to go before regaining his strength, the possibilities of complications had receded.

A wave of thankfulness overwhelmed her. She had never loved him so deeply, or with such compassion, as in that moment. It was a love that consumed her while bringing a tenderness she had never before experienced and, gently but compulsively, she bent down and pressed her lips against his forehead.

At that moment Vivien came into the room.

Lydia immediately stepped back from the bed without making a sound. Her heart quickened its beat, her body heated as she met Vivien's cold accusing stare.

'I was just going,' she whispered, and went silently to the door. Comment or explanation would lend importance and drama to the moment, and she had no intention of apologising for the familiarity.

'A fond farewell!' Vivien could not keep the sneer from her voice and dared not betray her annoyance and jealousy.

Lydia made no comment. Lance stirred, and she left.

Vivien went over to the bed and took Lance's hand.

'I—I thought Lydia was here,' he said, faintly bewildered.

Had he felt the touch of Lydia's lips? Vivien suppressed her anger and said in a low, indulgent voice, 'You've been dreaming. As you can see, only I am here, and I've been told I can't stay.'

Dreaming. Lance wondered why he should have dreamed that Lydia kissed his forehead. He didn't want to talk; he wanted to drift in that unreal world of imagination, thankful that his breathing was easier and his cough, too. It was good of Vivien to come again, and he gave her hand a squeeze of appreciation.

'I'm . . . better,' he murmured.

'Soon be home,' she said hopefully.

He closed his eyes.

Vivien knew she must not stay. Obviously Lydia had not talked to him, or he would have known she had been there. It seemed important that he should not remember her kiss. She would have to think of some scheme whereby Lydia confined her visits to practice discussions.

'I'll leave you to sleep,' she said softly.

'Good of you to come again. . . what time is it?' He had the frail, pale appearance of one who had been very ill and was on the way to recovery, but with always the possibility of a relapse.

'It's nine o'clock . . . goodnight, darling.' She bent and kissed him. 'See you tomorrow.'

But his eyes were closed.

As he drifted back to sleep, he could have sworn that Lydia had been there . . . kissed him. But of course, Vivien was right: he'd been dreaming. . . Nevertheless, he felt a little selfconscious as he saw Lydia the following lunchtime.

'Well?' he queried, after the questions about his condition had been discussed.

'I was called out in the night to your patient Mrs Grayson,' she said immediately.

'I promised faithfully I'd deliver her.' He looked anxious. 'How did it go?'

'Splendidly—a seven-pound boy. She accepted me with good grace.'

'No complications?'

'None. I had to do an episiotomy (an incision made at the bottom of the vagina to prevent tearing of the perineal tissue) and she's fine. She was very sorry to hear about you.' Lydia added, 'And sent all her good wishes.'

Lance looked pleased. 'We're lucky with our patients in the main,' he said, wondering if Lydia was as cool and collected as she seemed. She had taken on the extra load of work without fuss, or even a hint of complaint. He felt weak, restless and, suddenly, bloody-minded.

'I want to go home,' he muttered.

Lydia's hands were tightly clenched in her lap. It was exquisite torture to sit there, talking about work, having satisfied herself that he was progressing, yet be unable to express a single honest emotion.

'Your physician, Dr Phillips, wouldn't agree with you. And you'd tell your patients that it would take from seven to ten days to recover and then they'd need two to three weeks' convalescence. But for the Penbritin, you'd probably have had pleurisy and an infection of the right lung as well. The penicillins work wonders, and make people think they're stronger than they are.'

'I know how I am,' he retorted.

'And I know your chart. Your T.P.R. was alarming to begin with.'

'If I have any more fluids I shall float!' Lance protested.

'Your salvation.' Lydia knew him in this mood and wondered, even allowing for his physical condition, what had prompted it. 'You need building up.'

'And you talk like a doctor,' he said, suddenly relaxing.

'It has been known!' she laughed. But all the time she was waiting for Vivien to appear and she wanted to avoid seeing her.

'I'm very grateful, Lydia. Sorry you've been left to hold the fort.'

'I like a challenge,' she shrugged.

'You did offer to be an "emergency doctor",' he said unexpectedly.

Lydia recalled their conversation the evening before the disastrous party.

'Good heavens, fancy your remembering that!'

'There's very little I forget . . . Mr Barnaby,' he said *à propos* the statement.

'He died the night you came in here.'

Lydia looked around her. The atmosphere was pleasant, with turquoise-and-white curtains and chair covers. The nursing home was in Fitzjohns Avenue, standing in its own garden surrounded by sturdy Victorian houses, many of which had been turned into flats. She thought that life and death were always in curious juxtaposition in these rooms, and she studied Lance with a sudden thankful yearning, remembering the kiss she had given him and the shock of Vivien's arrival. The fact of being observed didn't worry her; if anything it awakened a defiance which emphasised the past. Nothing could alter the fact that she had been Lance's wife. In these medical surroundings she was at home, her rights inviolate.

Vivien arrived at that moment, and froze at the sight of Lydia.

'Don't tell me you're bothering Lance with work *again!*' She tried to make it sound lighthearted, but there was an edge to her voice. She kissed him with some deliberation and stood stiffly by the chair at the side of the bed, intimating that Lydia should vacate it.

'I was just going,' said Lydia as she got to her feet. 'I've got three visits before surgery—yours,' she added, smiling at Lance. 'I'll give you all the latest bulletins tomorrow.'

'Don't hesitate to call on Clive if it gets too much,' Lance suggested anxiously. He was still mystified as to why Lydia had been so emphatic about not marrying Clive.

Staff came in at that moment.

'Time to rest, Dr Richmond.' She noticed that Lydia was standing by the door.

Outside, in the corridor, Vivien looked straight into Lydia's eyes and said somewhat curtly, 'I want to talk to you, Lydia. There are matters we must discuss.' She paused and added significantly, 'In Lance's interests. I suggest this evening before you leave Carisbrooke and I return here.'

With that she moved on.

CHAPTER NINE

It was at tea-time that same afternoon that Nurse West's voice hailed Lance as he sat out in the armchair. 'I've brought you a visitor,' she said, revealing Hester.

'Hester!' There was delight in Lance's voice.

She stood there, her smile wide, her eyes full of compassion, as she moved in his direction and Nurse West guided her to a chair at his side.

Lance took both her hands and leaned forward to kiss her cheek in a rare gesture, his pleasure obvious. She shivered at his touch, her heart quickening its beat.

'I wanted to come before,' she confessed, 'but I know you had to be protected from visitors.' Her face was turned to his as though she was studying it intently, sensing as much as others saw.

'You look like a roseflin that soft pink dress,' he commented. 'Just the tonic I need . . . Ah, here comes the nurse with some tea . . . how did you get here?'

'Bunty drove me. I'm going to walk back—it's a perfect day.'

And, thought Lance, a long walk, but he was not indiscreet enough to say so.

Hester felt carefully around the tea-tray and picked up her cup which Lance had half-filled. Her movements were sure, delicate and deliberate.

'Your coming is just what I needed,' he admitted. 'Too much time to think in these places.'

'Pleasant thoughts are company,' she said gently, but she could feel the depression weighing upon him. 'But the getting better can sometimes be worse than when one is too ill to know. One sees everything out of proportion.'

'I spoilt the evening,' he said gently, and sighed ruefully, his voice was still weak.

'By worrying us.'

'You *knew*,' he said.

'Yes,' she agreed. 'People's voices tell me everything if I listen carefully enough.'

'Ah,' Lance exclaimed, 'the trouble is, we *don't* listen half the time.'

Hester sustained a note of boldness as she dared to say, 'You don't want a country cottage. . .why, Lance?'

He stared at her in amazement.

'What on earth makes you say that?' he asked incredulously.

'The instinctive feeling I had when it was mentioned—even allowing for your being ill.'

His voice was a little self-accusing. 'I'm in a rut. Vivien's quite right—we need a change of pattern. It's inevitable, in any case. My consideration, of course, is for the practice which mustn't be neglected because I choose to spend some weekends away. Patients come first.'

'Consultants very often live quite a distance from their rooms,' offered Hester.

'I'm a G.P., Hester. I should really live over the shop to give the very best service.'

'A partner could, in effect, do that and live, as you do now, on top of Carisbrooke.'

'Ah,' he said with feeling, 'I need a partner and an assistant if I'm going to get away with an easy mind.'

'You've been talking of getting a partner for a long while,' she reminded him, knowing that nothing she said would give offence.

'Vivien has emphasised that.' He added ruefully, 'Lydia and I have worked so well together.'

'Your marriage to Vivien will change all that,' said Hester with the latitude automatically accorded her.

Lance had always been able to talk to Hester about his emotional reactions to life. He wondered if her blindness—quite apart from her natural sympathy—enabled him to be completely unselfconscious, because she could not see his changing, or revealing expressions. Yet she had the uncanny knack of reading his thoughts.

'I know.' It was an abrupt agreement.

'A change of scene,' she said deliberately, 'helps adjustment. I was right—you're not enthusiastic.'

He sighed. 'Oh, Hester, you know me too well! But I've got to put the practice first.'

Hester sipped her tea.

'If we want a thing badly enough, we manoeuvre our plans so that we can get it . . . You would always make sure that the practice didn't suffer. There's no question in your mind on that point.'

He explained, '*I* suggested having a weekend place—'

'Without giving it serious thought?'

'Yes; I suppose I didn't realise how eager Vivien would be about it, or that she would want to get it immediately.'

'You'll stay in your present flat?' Hester asked.

'To begin with. . . Vivien has something larger in mind. At the moment I don't even want to move out of this chair. I'm in no mood to make decisions. . . It's good to think aloud, Hester. I can always do that with you. You're such an understanding person.'

'Your happiness means a lot to me,' she said quietly. 'You've been so good to me.'

'That's a privilege,' he said softly.

Hester sat there, aware of him with an intensity of feeling she could not control, knowing that he loved her with almost brotherly affection, and regarded her as part of the family. There were no barriers, and because she had adapted to the situation, no self-consciousness. If Lance committed murder he would, she felt, tell her of the crime. She did not want to take advantage of this bond in the present circumstances, but her view of his engagement was tormenting.

'Give yourself a chance to get stronger before you plunge into any decisions,' she suggested wisely. 'There are many houses in the country that would suit you.'

'Vivien is looking over the one at Windsor tomorrow, and Steven is going with her. The owners won't have any difficulty in selling.'

Hester's words tumbled out, 'I shall miss the weekends at Heath Edge.'

Lance looked shocked.

'Good heavens, it won't make all that difference, and you'll be able to come and stay with us,' he said confidently.

There was a rather tense silence.

'Vivien—'

'Vivien,' he said sharply, 'accepts my friends, as I should hers, had she made any, or had any, in London. It's unfortunate that they're scattered all over the world. Oh, no, Hester; the pattern may have to change, but certainly not to *that* extent. If I thought—' He stopped. He was on dangerous ground.

Hester put a hand on his coat sleeve and quickly drew it away as she said, 'When you're better, you'll have to face facts, Lance. And deal with them.'

She was prepared for an explosion, but all he said was, his voice low and subdued, 'I know. I know; but I don't want to *see*. And you're the only person in the world I could say that to.'

At that moment Clive came into the room, showing instant pleasure at the sight of Hester, and having spoken to her said to Lance, 'I'm told you're making good progress . . . I've just seen Matron. We've got an angina case in here.'

Lance found himself studying Clive intently. What had happened between him and Lydia to make her so emphatic about not marrying him? A mutual understanding? A simultaneous change of heart? He was perturbed because emotions seemed so completely unpredictable. He cursed the fact that he himself had been ill; it had taken the edge off his engagement, and where he and Vivien would have been celebrating . . . His thoughts stopped there abruptly and he plunged into conversation with Clive, stating, finally, that he was going home on Sunday, his restlessness obvious. He had made the decision even as he talked to Hester, maintaining that he could take things easily as well there as sitting in that room brooding over his inactivity and seeing things out of proportion. Hester had given him a platform from which he could proclaim his forebodings and, in the process, restore his hopes. He realised that no future could be built on the ashes of the past, and it was the future he had to face now. Once he was home, the depression would vanish instead of lying like a weight crushing his chest and preventing him thinking rationally.

Clive did not resist the idea of Lance returning home, but he said, 'I'd like to suggest you get some sea air.'

Lance thought of escaping to the sun. He and Vivien could . . . He retreated. He certainly could not leave Lydia without any moral support in the practice.

Lance laughed. 'The doctor's palliative. . . What I want is to get back to work; that's the best tonic.'

'If you won't go away, then Heath Edge is the place for you. A garden to sit or lie in; and the Heath for walking as you gradually get fit. No good your going back to the flat.'

Lance felt awkward. Vivien was intent upon his returning to Connaught Square where she could join forces with Mrs Carson and hasten his convalescence. Going to Heath Edge would seem a rejection of all her sympathy and good intentions. He consoled himself that he would talk to Marion when she came in later on. Edward had a hospital committee meeting and she would be alone, so he could take her into his confidence.

Clive said to Hester when it was time to leave, 'I'll run you home; we're both going the same way and I've a little free time until an appointment at six-thirty.'

'Oh, splendid,' Lance said immediately. 'Far too hot for walking today,' he added quickly, so that Hester would not lose her feeling of independence.

Clive saw Hester into her flat some short while later. Bunty appeared, and left them alone together in the sitting room.

Hester sat silent and subdued for a minute longer before she said brokenly, 'He's unhappy, Clive.'

Clive moved and sat beside her on the sofa.

'He's been ill,' Clive stressed. 'The depression is part of it.'

'I don't mean that,' she corrected. 'You see, he isn't the type of man to have a broken marriage and a broken *engagement*.'

'But he's only just become engaged.'

Hester felt that her courage and strength were ebbing away. Love, hurt, unhappiness overwhelmed her. Her usual strength deserted her.

'I want him to be happy,' she whispered brokenly.

Clive understood. He put his arm around her shoulders as he murmured, 'Oh, Hester, my dear!' Their pain was shared.

Tears fell unchecked from her sightless eyes.

'I'm sorry,' she gulped, 'I don't cry, or behave like this. There are so many things the blind have to conceal in case people think they're unhappy. We daren't do anything that begs for sympathy. You're different—'

He tightened his grip and held her with a firm gentleness that made her cling to him and then draw back, catching her breath as she did so, rather like a child.

They were two people enduring the same emotions, their situations parallel, unrequited love a torment.

'We can't live the lives of those we love, protect them from unhappiness,' Clive said quietly, 'or save them from their own follies.'

He thought of Lydia. He was as helpless to help her as Hester was to spare Lance. He had no illusions about Vivien, or how subtly she must have manoeuvred the engagement.

He looked at Hester, touched by the sadness of her face and what seemed suddenly a poignant helplessness.

She held his hand for a fraction of a second.

'Thank you,' she whispered. 'And forgive me for being so weak. He looks so drawn . . . if he'd been well—'

'I know,' he said softly. 'And I'm so sorry—'

'It's helped,' she told him, sighing and squaring her shoulders as one making a resolution.

'We'll go to La Bella Rosa tomorrow evening,' he said suddenly. 'Do us both good.'

'Dear Clive,' she said, and there was a world of gratitude in her voice.

'This is a bond.' He picked up her hand and kissed it, then got to his feet.

Hester raised her face and he looked down at her with infinite tenderness.

'I'll ring you about the time for tomorrow,' he said.

She walked beside him to the front door. No more words were spoken and none was necessary as she stood and waited, listening to the sound of his car driving away.

The loneliness had gone from her suffering.

'In Lance's interests'.

The words were drummed in Lydia's brain as she waited for the last surgery patient.

What matters were there to discuss? She felt empty, tense and apprehensive, and suddenly her kissing Lance held significance. Suppose he had been aware of it and had discussed it with Vivien? Colour flamed into her cheeks; her temperature seemed to soar into the hundreds . . . Surgery; patients. Mrs Wentworth wouldn't make an appointment unless it was urgent. She was the ideal patient, who used her common sense and 'sent for the doctor' at the right time.

She was a very slim woman, fair, thirty and smartly dressed. When she sat down she said honestly, 'I feel terrible, Dr Richmond, and I've a really dreadful pain all round my right side near my breast. It's a new pain, as though someone were tearing my skin off, and it tingles.'

Lydia examined her.

'You've had this for two or three days,' she said sympathetically.

'Yes; I thought it was "nothing" and would. . . oh, you know.'

'I know,' Lydia agreed with understanding. 'Doctors are the very last people we want to see! A love-hate relationship . . . you've got shingles.'

'Oh, no!' Mrs Wentworth added, 'It can drag on and—'

'The blisters are only just beginning to show; with an antiviral drug,' Lydia said encouragingly, 'we can prevent post-herpetic neuralgia and reduce the length of the attack.'

She wrote out a prescription for Herpid. 'Apply locally with the applicator brush, four times daily,' she said, 'and I've given you some pain-killers. Believe me, I don't underestimate the pain.'

'It *is* hell,' Mrs Wentworth admitted.

'And avoid spreading chickenpox, by not mixing with children or anyone who hasn't had it,' Lydia warned.

'The twins are away at school and they've both had chickenpox. So has my husband. I don't feel like mixing with people at the moment.'

'I'm sure you don't.' Lydia added, 'Also, avoid powdery lotions, they irritate the places where the blisters have broken. . . cool baths help.'

She thought as Mrs Wentworth left her that sometimes the word 'agony' was not an exaggeration to describe the pain of shingles.

Vivien came into Lydia's room at the end of the day. The house had emptied of most of its occupants; waiting rooms were deserted; staff on the way home. Her mood was conciliatory, but her smile artificial.

'I don't want to be misunderstood,' she began. 'My anxiety to talk to you has nothing to do with the little scene I witnessed at the nursing home. I may as well be honest: I know you're still in love with Lance, which doesn't make my position at this moment any easier.'

Lydia said with cool admonition, 'My feelings for Lance are not a subject for discussion, Vivien. You can't possibly judge them, anyway. Suppose you come to the point? You spoke of this being "in Lance's interests".' She paused, then added, 'I suggest you enlarge on that.'

'Very well . . . I'm sure you realise that he isn't making as quick a recovery as one might hope. The—'

'It isn't quite a week,' Lydia pointed out. 'He was very ill to begin with and he's got to pick up; his condition is following a normal course. If anything, he shouldn't be asked to make decisions, or be worried by buying houses,' she added pointedly.

'I see,' Vivien said icily. 'Naturally the last thing you want is for him to spend even a part of his time out of London.' She added swiftly, 'But I didn't come here to discuss *our* personal affairs, but to ask you to help him by making things easy.'

Lydia stared at her aghast.

'I don't understand. I've done all I possibly can in the practice—set his mind at rest.'

Vivien gave her an amazed stare.

'How true! You just *don't* understand, do you? You can't see how difficult Lance's position is where you're concerned? He's been wanting to break away—end your association—and this situation, now, is heaping coals of fire upon him, as it were. He's worried sick and admits that he hasn't the nerve, or the courage, to tell you the truth. As he said to me the other evening, "Lydia has been splendid this week; how can I say, thank you very much, but I want to replace you and I already have a partner in mind?" He's depressed and trapped.'

Lydia's heart felt like a wound in her chest; sickness washed over her and she shivered in the heat.

'I'm sorry,' Vivien told her. 'I assure you I'm thinking only of him, and worried on his account. He's too soft-hearted a person to betray his feelings. Your visits, other than in connection with work, have been a strain, too; but again, he can't possibly ask you to confine them to professional matters. And I can't tell him why you've been there so much. And don't think his reactions have been solely on account of our engagement. The anxiety, he confessed to me, has been there for some time. The question of "how to get rid of Lydia without hurting her". I've an idea, too, that he suspects you still have a soft spot for him, although that side of it's not been mentioned. It's been a great blow to him that you've not become engaged to Clive.' Vivien paused and sighed. 'He'd counted on that, and delayed making an issue of your practice association, believing the problem would solve itself.'

Lydia felt that every word was a nail being hammered into her flesh.

'Your concern,' Vivien went on, 'for him this week . . . He's in a doubly difficult position now. It's worrying him desperately, and I'm helpless. You *must* see, Lydia?'

There was a heavy silence; a dangerous silence, while Vivien sat tense and hopeful.

And suddenly, the words echoing like thunder, Lydia's mood changed; the stabbing pain, the sick disillusionment vanished before determination and courage, as she said, her voice strong, attacking, 'Oh, I see, Vivien; I see perfectly. It's you who want me out of the way, not Lance; and this is your devious method of forcing me out, counting on my pride and concern for him, to achieve your objective.'

Vivien bristled. There was fear in her eyes which glistened like steel. 'Nothing of the kind! If you're so thick-skinned—'

Lydia said forcefully, 'I was once Lance's wife, and there are certain things about his character that I know beyond all doubting when it really comes to it. I know he wouldn't pretend to me about our association. In our marriage, and since, there's always been frankness between us. We've never made any secret of the fact that we've enjoyed working together, and when he no longer wishes to do so, or has reason for severing the relationship, he'll tell me so face to face, not go talking about getting rid of me—talking behind my back.'

A dark anger, mixed with fear, crept into Vivien's expression, as she snapped, 'Wouldn't you like to believe that? Wouldn't you? You don't know Lance; you couldn't even stay married! But you're a dog-in-the-manger, now that you know he's fallen in love with me and wants me to be his wife you can't take it; you're going to hang on until the last moment, endure every indignity rather than believe the truth!'

Lydia's heart was thumping, but because of the conviction of her emotions and the strength of her purpose, she said, 'I *know* the truth. It doesn't matter whether married people agree or don't agree, there's something between them that, no matter how they part, that knowledge remains. It's a bond, if you like. If the two people remain friends, then that friendship holds something that's inviolate. It doesn't matter, also, when they fall in love again, live ideally happily married lives. "The Moving Finger writes; and, having writ, Moves on: nor all thy Piety nor Wit Shall . . . wash out a Word of it". Omar Khayyám's words . . . And when you've been married to Lance you will remember *my* words . . . so don't try to tell *me* that Lance would behave in a manner foreign to everything he stands for. It isn't a matter of perfection. A man may be unfaithful, lie, cheat, if you like, but he can never change certain facets of his character, any more than a strawberry can become a raspberry.'

Vivien sat there, staring, aghast.

'You must read a lot of romantic novels,' she said ridiculingly, while struggling to conceal her anger. 'And what have you to say about his attitude over your relationship with Clive?'

Lydia didn't hesitate. 'I think you've put your own interpretation on it.' She felt emotion stabbing. 'I can well imagine Lance's saying that he was sorry Clive and I couldn't get together. As a matter of fact it *would* have solved the problem of my professional association with Lance. I should then have joined the Hampstead practice.'

'I wonder you don't marry Clive; he seems interested in you,' Vivien said condescendingly, 'but then I suppose you secretly delude yourself that Lance still cares for you?' Anger blazed in her eyes.

'No,' Lydia said quietly and with dignity, 'I don't think that. Lance isn't the type of man to become engaged to one woman while loving another.'

The words fell on a tense silence; the room was suddenly and uncannily still.

'But,' Lydia went on, '*you* don't love *him*. There's only one person you love, Vivien—yourself. You're marrying Lance for financial reasons, and because you think he'll meet all your demands. You've started immediately with the cottage, and persisted even while he's been ill—'

'We've only an option for a week,' Vivien rushed in.

'There are other cottages . . . you think you'll be able to mould his life, have your own way. Don't underestimate him.'

'And of course you know!' The remark fell indiscreetly.

'Yes,' said Lydia with an amused smile.

'And you're so bloody clever!'

Lydia got up from her desk.

'I'm going to the nursing home,' she said firmly.

Vivien, red-faced, defeated, raised her voice. 'And if I see any more touching little love scenes,' she warned, 'I shall tell him, and make you look a pathetic fool!'

'And yourself a jealous spiteful woman whom he'll despise,' said Lydia with a quiet conviction. 'You have nothing to fear from me, Vivien, and if it will set your mind at rest, I shall certainly not be in the picture after you're married. This elaborate pretence was quite unnecessary, I assure you.'

'You mean you're going away?' There was overwhelming relief in the words.

'You'll know my plans in good time,' Lydia told her, with an air of dismissal.

Lance's convalescence was slow. He went to Heath Edge, Dr Phillips insisting that he didn't return to the flat and needed fresh air. Vivien suggested that they went to Europe to the sun, but Lance hadn't the energy to travel and was content to lie out in the garden on the hammock and, contrary to all his normal inclinations, do precisely nothing. His blood pressure was low, his pulse slow. People tired him and he found Vivien's continual planning exhausting. He had flatly refused, when it came to it, to buy the Windsor house and be rushed into a folly he might regret. Vivien excused her unseemly precipitateness as being eloquent of her overwhelming desire to establish roots, and the challenge of the short option had, she maintained, further stimulated her interest.

Inevitably there came the day when Lance was fit and back at Carisbrooke, working with renewed vigour and welcomed warmly by his patients, who were nevertheless full of praise for Lydia.

'You certainly held the fort with flying colours,' Lance said to her at the end of his first week back, when the long shadows of September crept over the gardens and mists rose from the countryside.

Lydia was trembling, emotion making every nerve tense, her heart thumping as she exclaimed, trying to keep her voice steady, 'I don't want to pry, Lance, but may I ask when you think of getting married?'

He was standing by the window of his consulting room and he swung round to face her, his body stiffening, his expression resistant. 'Why do you ask?' His words came deliberately.

'Because my own plans are involved,' she said quietly, meeting his gaze and then looking away.

'*Your* plans?' he echoed. 'How?'

All the air seemed to have gone from the rooms as she said, 'Because when I leave here, I don't want to inconvenience you; but I'd like everything settled.'

The silence was electric. They stared at each other in a kind of speechless questioning.

Lance moved and sat down rather heavily at his desk, arms folded across his large blotting pad.

'I seem to have been out of the real world for far longer than a few weeks,' he said. 'I honestly don't know when we're getting married. I haven't been in the mood to—to plan.' His voice dropped and then rose again as he said with what seemed an effort, 'But of course, you want to. . .' He paused, picked up his paper-knife and toyed with it as if for inspiration. 'It's difficult to imagine Carisbrooke without you,' he said unevenly. 'May I ask what you have in mind?'

'A country practice,' she said, the idea having just come into her head. Her thoughts were racing. She was remembering his kiss; their life together; their working here togther. 'The West Country—Somerset, probably.' She gave a little unnatural laugh. 'Depends on what's going. I want to put down some roots.'

Lance just stared at her and said, 'I shall miss you.'

Lydia felt the tears stinging her eyes and a lump rose in her throat. How was she going to keep up that calm conversational pose? She recalled Vivien's words about Lance wanting to get rid of her, and rejoiced that she had taken the stand she had, and not believed her. It would have seemed a gross disloyalty, and a tremor went over her, because she knew that what Lance had just said was sincere. Even if she were not in love with him, they would miss each other. Not even his engagement to Vivien could alter that, she told herself with some consolation.

'And,' she managed to say shakenly, 'I shall miss you.' She changed her mood to prevent breaking down. 'Now let's deal with plans. I don't like vague maybe's.'

He got up again from his desk and moved over to the chimney piece, his elbow on it, his head resting on his hand as he stood contemplating her.

'You mustn't be hampered be my arrangements,' he said with sudden gravity. 'I think Edward knows of somebody who would suit this practice, but we haven't discussed it at any length. I hardly chose the most opportune time to be ill! But,' he added, 'even if I got a partner it wouldn't necessarily mean your going.' He looked confused and avoided her gaze. 'I'm not expressing myself very coherently.'

There was bewilderment in the look they exchanged.

'But I know what you mean,' Lydia said swiftly. 'Had I wanted to stay, I could.'

'Exactly.'

'There was never any question of my doing so, Lance.' She added genuinely, 'And Vivien would have every reason to object. There are limits.'

As she uttered those words Lydia felt she had reached those same limits. He stood there, his attraction overwhelming, and his uncertainty bringing a curious element of vulnerability as though he were defeated by circumstances and bewildered by his own reactions.

'There's no point in our delaying our marriage,' he said with sudden finality. 'But I agree that it would be a good idea if we made a specific time so far as *our* association is concerned—the end of—'

'The locum!' she rushed in, emotion like a fire tormenting her. She longed to be in his arms; she wanted his lips on hers, his body hard against hers. Not for him to be standing stiff and suddenly unapproachable as he talked of his marriage to another woman.

Lance straightened his back and moved into the centre of the room.

'The end of October,' he said, 'if that's agreeable to you?'

'Quite. I shall take a holiday before I start again.'

'You need one now,' he said ruefully. 'I don't underestimate how damned hard you've worked. Thank you, Lydia.' His voice was low. 'For everything.'

A knock came at the door and a second later Vivien stood there.

'Mrs Trent said it was all right to beard you in your den, darling,' she said to Lance, giving Lydia a cursory glance.

Lydia seized the opportunity. 'You've arrived at an opportune moment—I've just arranged with Lance to leave here at the end of October.'

'What?' It was an incredulous sound. Not being trustworthy herself, Vivien could not conceive of anyone else keeping his, or her, word. She added hurriedly, 'You'll be missed.' She looked from face to face. Lydia met her gaze with a dignity that made Vivien feel small.

The thought uppermost in her mind was how she could persuade Lance to marry her before Lydia left. That would increase her triumph.

CHAPTER TEN

THE atmosphere in the practice changed noticeably after the decision had been made about October. Mrs Trent, Julie and Nurse Webster were taken into Lance's confidence, and they looked almost forlorn at the news of Lydia's departure. They had known the engagement would change the pattern, but had not expected that change to come so soon. And as far as Vivien was concerned, their opinion had not altered; if anything, it had deteriorated since her attitude had become even more patronising.

'Well,' said Julie, 'that's the end of our hopes! If this had been a novel, they would have remarried and lived happily ever after. Somehow I never saw Dr Lydia leaving.'

'Her coming here,' said Mrs Trent practically, 'was purely temporary, to help Dr Richmond out. I think we're being a little—well,' she flushed slightly and added, 'romantic.'

'If I could like Miss Wayne I'd be happier,' Nurse Webster admitted. 'She's a—a—well, *managing* person. Devious.'

Julie exclaimed, 'Couldn't get him out of London quickly enough at the weekends! Hardly got the ring on her finger. Funny business, that cottage. I'm glad he wouldn't play. I reckon he's heading for the divorce courts again before he's even reached the registrar!' she added with a rueful smile.

'*Julie!*'

'You always say, *"Julie"*, when you agree with me but don't want to.'

Mrs Trent knew she was right.

'Anyway,' she exclaimed, trying to sound severe, 'it's none of our business, and that's our doorbell.' She shooed them back to their respective tasks as though they were chickens.

Julie had the last word as she was moving away. 'Dr Richmond and Dr Lydia have become very formal with each other. It can't be an easy position.'

And it wasn't an easy position. Where Lydia had expected Lance to continue in his relaxed familiar fashion, she found him somewhat stiff and withdrawn, even formal. The discussions revolved solely around patients and he didn't take her into his confidence where Vivien was concerned. It was as though a book had been closed and locked away. She wished she could escape, but knew she could not go back on the agreed date which, although only a matter of weeks away, seemed more like years. Vivien meanwhile thrived, her manner and expression selfsatisfied to the point of conceit. She spoke to Lydia when they accidentally met, but with an air of dismissal in her manner. Lydia's depression seeped within her like the old-fashioned London fog, and no amount of courage and determination could make her smile other than in a forced and distracted way. She was grateful for work and made visits that were not strictly necessary, much to the delight of her patients.

'You're overworking,' said Lance after surgery. 'Mrs Smith told me you called on her last evening and "how kind it was of you". It wasn't—'

She cut in, her voice cool, 'Mrs Smith had had a nasty bout of gastro-enteritis which has left her very weak, and her blood pressure's too high. Do we have to ration our visits?'

He sat there, powerful and, ironically, the more attractive because of his overt criticism. It was refined torture to meet his gaze and try to fight the emotion it aroused. Lydia thought desperately that they were two people who had nothing further to say to each other, their paths leading in entirely different directions. His future, she reflected with heartache, was secure; her own uncertain, empty of love. She thought of Clive with a degree of nostalgia. He knew she had nothing but friendship to give him and, sadly, they had drifted apart because, she suspected, he did not want to embarrass her by his attentions. He was sufficiently understanding to know how she would be feeling and, ironically, be able to put himself in her position. Life was a wilderness and she suddenly feared it, and her own inadequacy. She had done nothing about finding another locum job. She *would* have a holiday. She had promised Marion and Edward that, and their silent concern touched her. She had not been to Heath Edge, unable to bear Vivien's triumph and possessiveness. This was not a situation that could improve, or produce some miracle. She merely awaited the final blow of Lance and Vivien's marriage.

Meanwhile Lance was aware that a door had suddenly been shut between them which neither dared open, as he said, 'I think I've found a possible partner—an Andrew Cooper. He's been working with a colleague of Edward's. We'll have the usual six month's trial and probably get another assistant. We might end up as a group practice. No two people could have kept up our pace for very much longer.' He waited for her reaction.

Lydia struggled to overcome the sick regret that was gnawing at her, managing to say with enthusiasm, 'I'm so glad. I'd been concerned about your getting settled . . . I suppose we *should* have reached a point where we couldn't take on any more patients.'

'I've procrastinated,' he admitted. 'We could have got someone to join us—' He stopped. 'Pie in the sky.' He looked away from her and then spoke of a purely professional matter involving a patient, his distant manner returning.

Vivien broached the subject of marriage when Lance was about to leave her flat after they had dined at La Barola, a restaurant near Blandford Street.

'I hate these partings, darling,' she whispered. 'They're so—so—'

He looked distracted for a second and then he took her roughly in his arms, his kiss a little savage. He released her as he said, 'You're quite right.'

'Why don't we get married before Lydia goes?' she suggested, feeling that she was treading on eggshells. 'She won't mind taking over, with Clive and Edward's backing . . . she's very amenable. She told me she's looking forward to getting away from London and has no regrets at leaving the practice. It's all very amicable and—'

Lance said, icily outraged, 'I wouldn't dream of asking Lydia to take over while we—we went away, no matter who she had to help her. She's done enough recently,' he added, his expression grim. He lapsed into silence. '*No regrets at leaving the practice*'. He pulled himself up sharply. Did he want her to have?

Vivien kicked herself for her tactlessness and having made one blunder, plunged into another. 'I suppose it wouldn't be the thing to ask an ex-wife to hold the fort while her ex-husband went on his honeymoon with the second Mrs Richmond!' She gave a little high-pitched laugh.

Lance's stare was frosty. 'Suppose we leave the past out of it.'

She went close to him and said wheedlingly, 'I'm sorry, darling . . . I'm just thinking what a waste of time this waiting is in the circumstances.'

'I couldn't possibly get away now,' he temporised.

'You wouldn't have to get away,' she said persuasively. 'We could be married by special licence without any question of a honeymoon. I'd be with you, and that's all I care about. We don't have to be conventional about it, and of course the practice would have to come first. Nothing would, in effect, change except that you would feel you had my support. You could then start with your new prospective partner with everything smooth. Lydia wouldn't be asked to do anything extra. We'd just tell Edward and Marion, and then announce it as a *fait accompli*. I can see your point of view, and naturally you don't want a lot of fuss.'

Lance studied her intently. 'You'd be satisfied, content with that?'

'Yes,' she promised, and not wanting to be too undemanding, added, 'Providing that next year we have a special holiday. If you ask me, all this makes sense. We're not two romantic teenagers who must have all the trimmings. The important thing is being together.' She deliberately looked a little pensive.

'What is it?' he asked.

'I want everything to be different from—from the first time,' said Vivien a little falteringly.

Lance's face seemed expressionless as he said inscrutably, 'It will be.'

'You were married in church?'

'Yes.' It was a clipped utterance.

She left it at that, while resenting his reticence and the fact that she felt it would be indiscreet to pursue the subject further. She was not sufficiently emotionally involved to be jealous of Lydia, but afraid of her influence and the nostalgia she represented. It had angered her immeasurably because Lydia had refused to believe the distortions she had disseminated about Lance. Her cool incisive manner, her confidence in certain facets of his character, had awakened an inward fury that still lingered. She felt instinctively that were she to hint at any of Lydia's faults, he would be equally defensive. It was like fighting ghosts. But she was determined to have the present situation resolved.

'And you agree with my idea about our avoiding any fuss?'

'Yes,' he said without hesitation. 'It will mean living at my flat, Vivien. And at this stage I don't want to have to think about country cottages—I may as well be honest about that. I shall have quite enough readjustments to make with the practice, without haring around looking at properties! Later on, when the work-load is lighter, it would be a good idea.'

Vivien's voice was smooth and beguiling. 'Darling, it doesn't matter if we never have one. I was foolish over the Windsor place, but I honestly thought it would do you good to get out of London now and again . . . Please understand that I only want to be with you.'

Lance felt humbled.

'Then that's settled.' He drew in his breath. When it came to it, why should he want to wait until after Lydia had left? She would be visiting Heath Edge no matter what plans he made. The bonds between her and Marion were far too strong to be severed by distance, even if she went far away. In fact, he argued, he was making Lydia an issue, which was absurd. He said abruptly, 'Only one thing—and I said this before, when you talked of our slipping away and being married secretly—I don't want any secrecy. I shall certainly tell Lydia.'

Vivien clenched her teeth before saying, 'Whatever you wish, darling. It doesn't matter.' She curved into his arms as she spoke. He held her and told himself that he had made a wise decision. There was nothing to wait for.

They fixed the date for Saturday, October the twenty-fifth. It was a weekend when Lydia was on call and would therefore not impose any extra work, or change the normal routine.

Vivien clung to him as he left the flat a little later. 'I shall make arrangements to leave my job just as soon as I can be replaced. There'll be no problems.'

The telephone rang at eight o'clock the following morning, just as Lydia had finished her breakfast, and Steven said, 'How about a meal this evening? It's ages since we had a gossip.'

Lydia didn't hesitate. 'Unless anything crops up. . . I'd like that. I didn't know we gossiped!'

'And I suppose you've heard the latest hot off the presses?'

'It's only eight o'clock and I haven't read the papers—what's news?'

'Lance and Vivien are getting married on October the twenty-fifth. She got me out of the shower to tell me!'

Lydia took a long deep breath and managed to keep her voice steady as she said, 'Really!'

It was strange how a date struck home. It was so final. But she was glad to know; she could face Lance much more easily now that she was forewarned.

He told her as they stood together in the common room, having a quick cup of coffee, but she made no mention of the fact that she alreay knew. It was an instinct never to repeat anything confided to her, no matter how innocuous.

'I think you're very wise not to waste time.' As he had explained their plans to have a delayed honeymoon the following year, she added, 'I would have been more than willing to hold the fort while you took a week off.'

He said, 'You're very generous, Lydia, but I wouldn't dream of it. I want Dr Cooper to start that week, while you're still here, so that you can steer him into the ways of the practice.'

She nodded her understanding and agreement, thinking painfully how very eager he must be to make Vivien his wife, since they were to be married when the practice would be going through such an upheaval.

'Nothing like having all the changes at once,' she said. Her gaze met his, lingered and then fell away. 'I'm having a meal with Steven this evening,' she said suddenly and somewhat briskly, 'so I must get on.'

He gave her a long enquiring look as they parted.

Mrs Trent caught up with Lydia as she was on her way out to do some visits.

'Miss Grey's mother has telephoned. Could you possibly call? Miss Grey's got a violent headache and can't get to the surgery.'

Lydia sighed and nodded.

Lance came alongside her. 'I heard that,' he said 'As far as I can see, you haven't stopped except for that coffee. I can imagine your being thankful to get into a practice in some peaceful spot where you have time to breathe.'

Lydia had the feeling that he was deliberately delaying her for no better reason than he wanted to talk; the withdrawn attitude having vanished because he could not sustain it.

'Country G.P.'s hardly have a rest cure,' she said, forcing a smile and taking a step forward.

'By the way,' he went on, 'I meant to ask you, how is our Mrs Hall—Trudy Hall?'

'The holiday in Rome was a great success. He seems to have got over his fugues. I think when she stayed out that time, and he probably thought she wasn't going to return, he learnt a lesson.'

'That he couldn't do without her,' Lance said quietly.

They looked at each other, aware of the significance of the remark.

'Enjoy yourself this evening,' he said irrelevantly. 'Steven's excellent company.'

Lydia said abruptly, 'When I come to reflect on it, leaving London would be a wrench. I value my friends, of whom Steven is one.' She looked reflective and then said quickly, 'I must go.'

Lance didn't move; just watched her.

Mrs Trent came towards him. 'A call for you, Doctor.'

He looked almost embarrassed and hurried towards his room.

Lydia reached the Grey flat which was in Crawford Street, aware that violent headaches could not be ignored. The Greys were comparatively new patients, and Brenda Grey, aged twenty, had only needed her attention once before. She was lying in a darkened bedroom, her mother, a plump sensible woman, whose husband was an electrician, worried, but not fussing.

'You see, Doctor, she's going to be married next week and all this has come on so suddenly.'

'Any vomiting?'

'No.'

Brenda was a beautiful girl with silken auburn hair and a matching fair skin which now had a ghostly pallor.

'I saw bright spots and zigzag lines when I woke up,' she managed to say, 'and when they went, I had this throbbing headache.'

Lydia made a routine examination and asked, 'Have you ever had this before?'

'No.'

'Was there any tingling, or numbness on one side of the face? Or hand, or leg?'

'No! Oh, doctor; I'm going to be married next week. . . I can't be like this. If it were just ordinary pain—' She stopped wretchedly. 'But it *isn't*. I couldn't do *anything*. . .Please help me!'

'This is a typical migraine,' Lydia said quietly. 'I can give you something to relieve the pain. In your case it shouldn't last very long.' She didn't say that it could last hours, or days; that the initial symptoms are brought on by the sudden narrowing of the arteries on one side of the head, and the headache follows when the same blood vessels widen again, allowing more blood to flow. Much research had been done and was being done as to why the blood vessels should contract in that manner.

'And you're not on the pill,' she said, 'so that couldn't be a contributory factor.'

'No,' came a whisper. 'I'm a virgin. Harvey and I— well, we agreed about it.'

Lydia found very few such cases. The pill could be a contributory cause in migraine, just as pregnancy often reduced the number of attacks.

'Usually,' she explained, 'the migraine starts after the stress is over. You would seem to go in reverse. I'll give you a prescription for Delimon—little white tablets. I can find nothing else wrong with you,' she added reassuringly. 'You should be better tomorrow.'

'I *must!*' Tears filled the large blue eyes. 'There's still so much to do, and we're going to Portugal for our honeymoon. I've never flown before and if I were like this. . . well, I—I couldn't even be married, let alone travel.' Brenda added hastily, 'And I *can* bear pain. I'm used to it at period times. . . I didn't bother to tell you that,' she admitted, 'when I first saw you when I had 'flu.'

'I normally ask,' Lydia admitted. 'We must see what can be done about that when you return. I'll look in tomorrow.' She wrote out the prescription as she spoke, and gave it to Mrs Grey on her way out.

Mrs Grey said hopefully, 'I've a feeling this will pass. Brenda's been working far too hard. They've wanted everything to be right. . . bought their own house and furnished it.' She added simply, 'They've got the right ideas about life. She probably needed a rest, and this is nature's way of giving it to her, painful though it is.'

Lydia was prepared to accept the convenient logic, and hoped she was right!

'I'll get the prescription made up so that she can—' The disciplined strength ebbed slightly, 'It would be so *dreadful* if anything should happen to spoil the day,' said Mrs Grey, her voice shaken.

Lydia put a hand on her arm.

'I don't think it will. She's young and strong. This is just one of those unfortunate things that occur from time to time. Migraine can be as unpredictable, as it can sometimes be predictable.'

'Thank you for coming so quickly, Doctor.'

Lydia left, and when she got back to Carisbrooke, Lance was in the reception area.

'Well?' he asked, looking at her with interest.

She told him.

'A migraine wouldn't be what the doctor ordered on a wedding day,' she said, adding, 'or any other day. She's petrified!' She sighed. 'One wants to perform miracles on these occasions. A happy family. This is only the second time I've seen them.'

'You care for your patients,' Lance said solemnly and on a note of admiration.

'Nothing can succeed if your heart isn't in it,' she said with conviction.

He was studying her as though making an assessment, and the intensity of his gaze was unnerving.

'You must get a partnership next time.' He added swiftly, 'In different circumstances you could have been mine, when you come to think of it.'

'I think that would have been carrying the civilised approach a little too far,' Lydia commented with a laugh. 'Incidentally, I'll be coming to Heath Edge this weekend. Hester will be there, too, as you know. I think Marion feels we should all get together for the last time before you're married. . . I must rush. I've letters to sign and a telephone call to make.' She managed to curb her emotion. 'You look like someone out of work,' she added as she hurried away before he had time to speak.

Hester switched off her talking book machine which was simple to use and had only three switches—on] off, volume control and track change, the books being recorded on to compact cassettes. It was a change from reading Braille, and there were over a thousand titles in the talking book library. She had lost concentration and was listening for the sound of Clive's car, for he had promised to look in on his way back from a patient in Belsize Park. She lightly traced her fingers over her face and said to Bunty, 'I feel sticky and I need some powder.' She added, a faraway look in her eyes, 'Lance telephoned when you were out shopping. . . he'll soon be married.'

'A good thing when it's over,' Bunty said practically, thankful that Clive had come into the picture recently, giving Hester a calmer, reconciled outlook.

Hester gave a little sigh.

'Yes,' she said quietly. 'One has to face things, and Vivien will see to it that he's alienated from his old friends. Much better to face the fact now. . . That's Clive.' There was relief in her voice. She would have been disappointed if anything had happened to prevent his coming.

Clive came in with the air of a man who was at home, finding his visits both soothing and inspiring because Hester's wisdom was profound in its simple truth, and they were able to talk on topics which would have embarrassed many people. They were also balm for each other's wounds.

'I'm not looking forward to this Sunday,' Clive confessed as they were settled and having a sherry. 'I'm rather surprised that Marion thought it a good idea.'

'Wouldn't it have looked rather pointed if she'd cut out Sundays altogether? We've not been there since the engagement.'

'Ah, but Lance being ill put things out, and the time has raced by.' He corrected that: 'It both races by and then, curiously, drags.'

'According to how we're thinking at the moment,' Hester said reflectively.

Clive nodded appreciatively, 'That's very true.'

Hester had made friends with her love for Lance during those weeks. He would soon be a married man again and she could not ignore her pride when it came to accepting Vivien. Lydia was different; she created a bond. Vivien destroyed any hope of one. Where Lydia would show compassion, Vivien would betray a certain contempt, as she had already done in a subtle fashion. There was no doubt that she suspected Hester's feelings.

'Mentally saying goodbye to someone can be very sad,' Hester mused. 'Coming to terms with one's emotions—'

'And accepting the fact that there can be new beginnings,' Clive said gently.

A tremor went over Hester as she sat there. It was like seeing a star suddenly on a dark night.

'Talking to you; knowing that you understand and that we have so much in common—' Her voice was shaky.

'It's been an oasis,' he admitted.

'Really, Clive?' There was a wistful expression on her face.

'Do you know what I think would bring us both happiness?' he said suddenly. 'And would be so right?'

There was a sudden tense silence.

'No—what?' It was a whisper.

'If we told them on Sunday that we were going to be married,' he said quietly, but formally.

'Married?' She caught her breath and turned her face to his.

'Will you marry me, dear Hester? Build a life with me? I'll do everything I can to make you happy.'

Almost shyly she slid her hand into his and felt the pressure of his fingers on hers.

'Yes,' she whispered.

They both knew that love had hurt and caused them heartache, but that now they had found a solace which would heal and remain with them forever.

CHAPTER ELEVEN

IT was one of those Indian summer days that held a beauty and mellowness heralding autumn, when Lydia joined the gathering at Heath Edge that Sunday. Marion saw her come into the hall and went forward, kissing her warmly; but there was a shadow behind her smile because she knew that the following week Lance would be married, and the more she saw of Vivien the more she feared for his happiness. In addition, she knew that all was not well from his point of view and that his distraction and faint air of depression was foreign. She had talked it over with Edward, who had warned her against discussing the matter, insisting regretfully that Lance knew his own business best, and interference might cause trouble and a possible rift. The wisdom of his advice did not, however, lessen his own concern.

'Don't go too far away, Lydia,' she begged. 'I'm being selfish, but even if we don't see a lot of you, you are *there*.'

'I always shall be,' Lydia promised, 'and I'm not going away yet. I haven't made up my mind about anything and I can't work up any enthusiasm. I may even go back into hospital life.' She saw the sadness in Marion's eyes and added wryly, 'Everything may work out far, far better than you expect. It's amazing what security does for some women, and I've an idea Vivien needs that.'

Lance came upon them as he was on his way to the patio, ice-cube container in his hands.

'I've never known any people who had so much to say to each other as you two!' he said spontaneously, looking from face to face. He added without thinking, 'It was always the same.'

Vivien's voice called from the sitting room doorway, 'What was always the same?' She smiled sweetly, but there was a note of interrogation in her voice.

Lance didn't hesitate, 'Marion and Lydia having such a lot to say to each other.'

She ignored that and exclaimed, 'Edward is waiting for the ice.' It was a rebuke.

Lance hesitated. There was a strange uncertain expression on his face. He looked at Lydia, noticing her navy-and-white skirt and blouse which had a brooch at the neck which he had given her on their wedding day. For a second he blinked as though unsure of himself, and Vivien said sharply, 'Lance! The ice—' She looked at Marion. 'Has he always wool-gathered?'

'No,' said Marion immediately, and went forward to greet Clive and Hester. Steven was already there.

Hester moved with sure steps, knowing every inch of the house. She looked beautiful, and there was an expression on her face of tranquility such as Marion had never seen before.

'I'd like a painting of you framed in the doorway and in that blue dress,' said Lance.

'So would I,' Clive agreed, and put his arm around her shoulders.

Hester raised her face to his questioningly; they instinctively moved closer.

'We're going to be married,' Hester said a little shyly.

Lydia, surprised, cried out first, 'Oh, I'm so glad!'

There was a chorus of good wishes as Edward and Steven came in search of the ice and they all hovered in the hall.

Clive looked at Lydia with the tenderness of farewell.

'Oh, Clive,' she said softly. 'All the happiness. I *know* you'll be happy.'

'I know it, too,' he agreed.

After the congratulations had died down, Vivien said, 'There must be something in the air to promote weddings among people who visit Heath Edge. And are you going to marry soon?'

'Before Christmas,' said Hester, her hand slipping surreptitiously into Clive's. She was safe and protected.

Lydia felt more lonely than she had ever done in her life. She was not a crying woman, but it would have been so easy for her to burst into tears and she swallowed hard, screwed up her eyes and took a deep breath. She didn't regret not accepting Clive, and was both thankful and relieved that he and Hester had found happiness together. She glanced at Lance, who at that moment turned and looked directly into her eyes. Emotion tore at her, memories flooding back. She plunged into conversation with Steven who said suddenly, and dramatically, looking at Edward and Marion, 'Would you excuse me if I have a word with Lance and Lydia alone? And, of course, you,' he added to Vivien.

Edward and Marion exchanged glances and murmured, surprised, 'No; no, of course not.'

Lance muttered something inarticulate, but led the way into the dining room, saying, 'What *is* it, Steven?'

Vivien ranged herself beside Lance. She paled as she saw the look of grim determination on Steven's face and cried out, *'Steven!'* Her voice was full of fear.

'I've been a cad long enough,' said Steven, 'and it doesn't matter if what I'm about to do is also caddish, but I can't contribute to misery when it's staring me in the face.'

Lance looked appalled. 'What are you talking about?'

'Us,' he said, glancing at Vivien, and there was contempt in his voice.

'No! No!' Vivien called out, and moved towards him, white, shaking.

Steven ignored her as he said, 'Vivien and I have been lovers for over two years—obviously during your engagement.'

Lance stared disbelievingly, then he exclaimed, his voice hardening, 'But—'

Vivien said swiftly, 'It isn't as it seems, Lance. . . I love you and—'

Steven's laugh was scornful, 'You love only one person—yourself!'

Just for a second Vivien's gaze rested in Lydia's and she heard the echo of Lydia's own words.

'But,' Lance asked harshly, 'why become engaged to me? Put up the elaborate pretence? Be so eager to be married, when all the time—'

Vivien stumbled as she tried to explain and Steven said quietly to Lance, 'You represented the security I had no intention of giving her. There was never any question of marriage: it has been a purely physical relationship which I despise myself for allowing to continue. The Windsor house was part of the plan. It would be near me and simple as a clandestine meeting place. I must have been mad to agree to such a scheme. I've no illusions, but I didn't realise that I was dealing with a woman who would stop at nothing to get what she wants, at no matter whose expense. Far better for you to be disillusioned now than to have all the misery later. You can't despise me more than I despise myself, but at least I've set you free.'

Vivien moved back to Lance's side.

'Forgive me,' she pleaded, 'it isn't as he says; he's jealous and he wants to—'

Lance thundered, '*Are* you lovers?'

She lowered her gaze and her silence was her condemnation. Then she turned like a tigress upon Steven. 'You're lower than I ever dreamed possible!' she grated through clenched teeth. 'If you'd wanted to get rid of me you could have done so—'

'And leave you to ruin Lance's life? No man likes failure twice,' Steven said quietly. 'A broken marriage and a broken engagement isn't easy to take. You knew that too. All you wanted was the ring on your finger.'

Lydia stood there, speechless, appalled, watching every shade of expression on Lance's face, unable to ignore what this twist of fate might mean and not daring to go beyond the moment. She was neither shocked nor surprised, because her instinctive distrust of Vivien made any eventuality possible. She looked at Steven sadly, not liking what she had heard, but respecting him for having had the courage to tell the truth.

There was a moment of heavy uncomfortable silence which Lance broke by saying with a bold determination, 'I can't play the hypocrite—the wronged fiancé.' He looked at Vivien and added, 'I was marrying marriage, cheating you and myself. I was never in love with you.'

'What!' Vivien's voice rose. Her pride and confidence vanished. She knew she had manoeuvred the engagement, been determined to secure for herself the kind of life she believed she could enjoy as Lance's wife.

Lance looked at Lydia and his words rang out with a clarity that spoke for itself. 'There's only one woman I love and have always loved; the woman I still think of as my wife.' He turned to Steven. 'I can't admire you for your behaviour, but I shall always be grateful to you for your honesty.'

Steven bowed his head for a second and then raised it with dignity.

'That's all I want to hear, because it was an instinct about your feelings which gave me the courage to face this—but I didn't expect you to be generous enough to admit it.'

Lydia sat down at the dining table because her legs would no longer support her. She dared not look at Lance.

And in those moments Vivien's world crashed. Her defiance, scheming and selfishness deserted her. She looked broken, abject.

Steven took her arm; pity stirred within him as he said, 'It's time we were leaving here. We deserve each other, but perhaps we can improve in the future.' He turned to Lance and Lydia in silent apology as he and Vivien walked out of the room and so from the house.

Alone with Lydia, Lance said quietly, 'Well, now you know the truth. I've been such a blind *fool*.' He looked at her in what seemed to be a never-ending gaze. 'When I kissed you. . . Oh, Lydia. . . how do you feel about me? Is there anything left from the past? Is it possible that—'

'Possible that I love you?' She moved towards him. 'The answer is yes.'

He gave a little cry and drew her into his arms, his lips at first gentle and wondering, and then possessive and demanding.

'Do you realise that we can't very well slip away now,' he said wryly, as they drew apart, eyes meeting as though they could not bear to look away.

She put her hand in his. 'But we can leave early,' she said, her eyes sparkling. 'I feel I'm living in a dream, anyway, and that any minute I shall awaken. . . darling, we must join them.'

'At least Steven protected Vivien from anyone else knowing. I shall just say that we'd made a mistake. . . I don't know how I'm going to make any sense,' he admitted.

'If you *will* want to make love to your wife,' she said, curving back into his arms.

'Desperately,' he whispered, his lips finding hers.

They went hand in hand out on to the patio. Edward and Marion, Clive and Hester, stared at them in astonishment.

'But Steven and Vivien have gone. We saw their cars—' Marion stopped. 'What is it?'

Lance looked from face to face. 'Shall we say there's been a broken engagement?'

'What?' There was no pretence, both Edward and Marion smiled as though they had suddenly come into a fortune.

'The ending of a chapter,' Lance told them. 'It wasn't a good book.'

Hester's voice, joyous and genuinely grateful, came in a moment of sudden silence, 'And you and-Lydia—'

'Divorce didn't suit us,' said Lydia, her gaze on Lance's face.

'You mean—' Edward beamed.

'We're going back to our little church to rectify the mistake,' Lance said, 'if my future second wife agrees.'

Marion's sigh was full of joy.

Edward said, 'This calls for champagne—' He looked at Clive and Hester with indulgent pleasure. 'Two marriages,' he said, and darted away like an eighteen-year-old.

Serenity had returned to Heath Edge.

An hour or two later Lance and Lydia arrived at the mews flat and Lydia handed him the doorkey.

'Home,' she whispered.

'Home,' he echoed, opening the door and closing it with determination. 'Thank God. . . if you knew how often I've pictured myself back here, my darling—'

' "My darling",' she repeated. 'They're like two words just discovered, and they sound like magic.'

'We were mad ever to be divorced,' he said almost roughly.

'And mad to think we ever could *be* divorced. We never were, really,' she said simply. 'You were always my husband in my heart.'

They were like two people savouring precious moments, listening to a stirring overture before the symphony began.

'Can you understand that I plunged into an engagement, refusing to admit that I was still in love with you?' he asked, and held her gaze with intensity. 'I couldn't endure the emptiness, the barrenness of life, and I thought you were going to marry Clive.'

'When it came to it, I couldn't compromise. Not that he didn't know of my love for you. He's a very understanding person who'll be far happier, eventually, with Hester than with me.'

Tension mounted; eyes looked into eyes, desire flaming. Lance took her in his arms and began to unzip her blouse. They didn't speak as they went into the bedroom. There was a dear familiarity about their undressing, together with the thrill of discovery after a time of separation and denial. Excitement and emotion increased as their bodies touched, and Lydia shivered with passion as his hold tightened, until ecstasy reached the climax of fulfilment. Eventually they lay still, clinging together as though afraid something might, even then, tear them apart.

A little worried frown gathered between her eyes, which he noticed and asked immediately, half fearfully, 'What is it, darling?'

'You once said we were sexually incompatible!'

He made a little apologetic sound. 'That was because I was trying to exorcise you—in the most extraordinary ways, I must admit.' He kissed the top of her forehead and cupped her breast. 'You've lost weight,' he said with a naturalness that added to the wonder of loving. 'I'd like to think it was through need of me.'

'It was,' she admitted honestly. 'Now I shall get fat with happiness and contentment.'

'Lydia?' He gave her name eloquence.

'Yes?' She spoke apprehensively.

'There hasn't been anyone since our divorce. The desire wasn't there.'

'Not for me, either,' she told him. 'My desire was for you.'

Lance gave a little whimsical laugh.

'Perfectly proper to desire one's husband!'

'But you were no longer my husband.'

'Ah,' he said, his lips on her cheek, 'there are some marriages that no divorce can dissolve. When will you marry me again, Mrs Richmond?'

She lifted herself on one elbow and looked down at him as he lay against the pillows, realising anew his strength and the power of his attraction.

'Just as soon as it can be arranged! I want us to have a special anniversary present next year,' she added, a hint of merriment in her eyes.

'Such as?' He held her hand as he spoke.

'A boy or a girl. . .'

And with that she lay down again, her head on his shoulder.

Doctor Nurse Romances

Incurable romantics, read one before bedtime.

Josephine, Jane and Jacinth were a trio of friends who as students at the Princess Beatrice Hospital in London shared the first years of hard work, laughter and tears.

But now the training is over and the time has come for them to go their separate ways as fully fledged nurses and midwives.

Take Three Nurses is a series of three stories that follow the individual fortunes of each of the three girls on the road to success and romance.

Josephine and a Surgeon of Steel

Jane and the Clinical Doctor

Jacinth and The Doctor Make a Wish